ROMULUS

A Novella from 19th Century Haiti

Fernand Hibbert

Translated from French and Kreyòl
by Matthew Robertshaw

Deux Voiliers   *Aylmer*
Publishing   *Quebec*

First Edition

Copyright of Translation © 2014 by Matthew Robertshaw

Published by Deux Voiliers Publishing, Aylmer, Quebec.

www.deuxvoiliers.com

Library and Archives Canada Cataloguing in Publication

Hibbert, Fernand
[Romulus. English]
    Romulus : a novella from 19th century Haiti / Fernand Hibbert ; translated from French and Kreyòl by Matthew Robertshaw.

Translation of: Romulus.
Includes bibliographical references.
ISBN 978-0-9881048-9-1 (pbk.)

    I. Robertshaw, Matthew, 1985-, translator II. Title.

PQ3949.H5.R6613 2014   843'.912   C2014-900048-0

Cover Art and Design by Matthew Robertshaw

Cover Photograph by Kate Ayalogu.

Red Tuque Books distributes Romulus in Canada. Please place your Canadian independent bookstore and library orders with RTB at www.redtuquebooks.ca

For Kiersten Robertshaw
and Cadieu Hibbert

Acknowledgements

Thanks to Joubert Satyre, Rocky Penate, Beth Fisher, Tessa Hawkins, Ian Shaw, Carrol F. Coates, Karen Racine, Victor Fernandez, Paul Plato, Joan Sider, Constance Garnett and Fernand Hibbert.

Foreword

Since the bicentennial of its independence in 2004, and particularly since the devastating earthquake of 2010, Haiti has been on our minds. But ask the man in the street what he knows about the country and he will typically utter something about the "poorest in the Western hemisphere," "foreign aid vs. political corruption," or maybe "Voodoo." Rifle through the international section of any newspaper and you'll likely see a picture of Bill Clinton or some other white diplomat promising to bring measurable change by some undetermined date. On the whole, here in the First World our insight into the day-to-day lives, the history and the culture of the developing world is marginal at most. Why then—as our world gets smaller, as our cities embrace multiculturalism, as the plastic artefacts of our material and media culture find their way to the remotest ports —why do we know so little about the anonymous majority of the world? Port-au-Prince, after all, is barely a thousand kilometres from Miami.

Did you know, for example, that in 1789, Haiti (then Saint-Domingue) was arguably the most profitable colony *in the world*? Did you know that when they declared their independence in 1804 they were *the second nation* in the New World to do so? Were you aware that, despite mass illiteracy, for the century-and-a-half after independence Haiti produced more books per capita than *any other nation* in the Western Hemisphere save the United States? In 1956, literary critic Edmund Wilson wrote about this thriving print culture: "the literature of Haiti…is highly sophisticated and has a long and sound tradition."[i] Be it poetry or prose, they have their masters.

So where did this sophisticated tradition come from?

The modern state of Haiti came about under a host of unique circumstances, and these circumstances have encouraged a literary heritage that is equally unique. Partly, their history and literature have been shaped by a perceived need to prove themselves to the world. The new republic of former slaves stood against everything that the nineteenth century empires were built on. First-generation Haitians were painfully aware of their responsibility to prove the fallacy of the racial ideologies of the day. They became obsessed with the idea of successfully running their state and proving to the world they were more than just *"gilded Negroes,"* as Bonaparte disdainfully dubbed them.[ii] Their literary elite, that ever-present and ever-miniscule group, also fell into this mindset of insecure endeavours—and in literature insecurity is not always detrimental (think Kafka, think Hemmingway).

This literary circle, many of whom were educated in post-revolutionary France, lived in a nation founded on ideas of individual liberty, political self-determination and racial equality that surpassed, even scandalized, the progressive minds of Europe. Haiti, since adopting the name, has been a place where the abstract ideas of liberty and equality are felt—in spite of, or perhaps because of, the persistent threat of losing them. Time and time again foreign powers and native authoritarian leaders have sought to dominate the people of Haiti, but they hold their resolve, they've done so for over two centuries, they will not be slaves again. Ideas of liberty, which in the developed world often become mundane and theoretical, still mean something in Haiti. This comes across clearly in their literature.

Another aspect of their culture that lends itself to their literature is the idea of heroes in Haitian society. The Revolution comprised a dramatic series of events, which brought several charismatic leaders into power. These men became a virtual pantheon of Haitian history, and subsequent leaders would attempt to espouse this superhuman status in their own political image. Haitian politics have been plagued with personality cults. For better or worse, the Haitian people have a keen appreciation for heroes and heroic tales.

If they have such a profound and sophisticated body of work then why haven't we heard of it?

We're ignorant to Haiti's literature for the same reason that we're ignorant to its history: the West has consistently tried to forget the place. Historians are to blame. For almost two centuries (they're getting better these days) when historians mention the Haitian Revolution, it's as a footnote to the Age of Revolution. In actuality it was the most radical, the most revolutionary of all. Why the silence? Precisely because it was so revolutionary, so "unthinkable." The Revolution was, until the second half of the twentieth century, typically demoted to the status of a 'rebellion' or a 'revolt,' ignored because it pointed to themes of slavery, colonialism and race, which, though critical to the existence of the Modern West, have largely been ignored in French history. Western history generally has also neglected these themes until recent decades; only with the increased interest in race beginning in the 1970s has the academic study of Haiti come to maturity.[iii]

Ultimately, Haitian poverty and non-development sealed the fate of the world's perspective on the Haitian Revolution. How could it be so significant if it led to such an impoverished society? It's tempting to think of it as a failed movement, but it isn't. The government has indeed struggled to find its feet, but the success of a revolution can't be measured exclusively by the government it produces. Their success transcended their borders. As the vanguard of the decolonization era, Haiti became a rallying point for subsequent Latin American, and later Africa, quests for independence. They welcomed runaway slaves and exiled revolutionary leaders with open arms.[iv]

As proponents of black dignity they were pointed out by abolitionist in Europe and the United States. Frederick Douglass, who became U.S. ambassador to Haiti after the Civil War, declared that they had "struck for the freedom of every black man in the world."[v] They stood up and told the declarers of the Rights of Man that they were in fact men. They defeated the armies of three European empires and established a modern liberal republic—their humanness was now incontestable. Pseudo-scientific racial classifications and draconian ideas of 'natural conditions' began to fall out of favour; world over, the ideological basis of slavery began to weaken.[vi]

Not to say they built a democratic utopia. The champion of the Revolution, Jean-Jacques Dessalines, named himself emperor for life (a pattern that others would follow in 1811 and 1849). Numerous presidents, too, after serving an appointed term, declared themselves leaders for life. For their rivals the ubiquitous coups d'état seemed the only option. Intense rivalry meant a continuous breakdown of political discourse. Literature filled the gap.

This was the tumultuous situation in which Fernand Hibbert wrote *Romulus* in 1908. An overarching theme is an appeal to discourse. Hibbert's voice seems to come most clearly through the character of Etienne Trévier, the hardworking merchant who starts off hopeful for Haiti's future but insists that the government must find some stability in order for the country to succeed. With four military coups since 1988 Hibbert's call for peaceful resolution is as pertinent as ever.

The pertinence of *Romulus* is indicative of a more general pertinence of the whole body of Haitian literature. Its universal themes of freedom and equality are timeless and its unique perspective is valuable. Yet only a fraction of the corpus has been translated. This is incongruous with, for example, the global interest in Latin American literature since the 1960.[vii] In wrapping up this project, and as I look forward to translating other works, I'm reminded of a twenty-nine-year-old British woman who, in 1891, pregnant and in poor health, passed her time learning Russian. She continued under the tutelage of a revolutionary anarchist who had fled to London, and ended up bringing the great works of Dostoevsky, Chekhov, Gogol and others to the attention of the English-speaking world.[viii] These classics of Russian literature were pertinent in the early twentieth century, just as the great works of Haiti are pertinent today.

Prologue

IN THOSE DAYS, Miragoâne was a prosperous and lively town. Her seniors were affable, her women light-hearted, her youths dreamers. At any hour, when you would walk down Main Street and the Seaside Road or if you passed through the side streets cross-cutting these main arteries, you would hear the fresh voices of women, young and old, as they sang their ballads—or more often, Alfred de Musset's ballad: *Rappelle-toi*.

On the Islet, in the neighbourhood with the billiard cafés and the grocery stores, the important gentlemen of the little town—that is to say the public officials in charge and the citizens who aspired to replace them—were gathered at the home of Sulla the hatter, the former harbourmaster-turned-café owner. And there, opposite the sparkling blue sea, beneath the benevolent breath of the faithful breeze, the stories, always the same, began again.

Ah yes! If ever there was a corner of the blessed world where happiness could be found among the human herd, it was here, in Miragoâne at the start of 1883. She was fragrant with freshness and illusion. Built with spirit, her halls went up left and right. Her young folks made promises and squabbled with the priest. As for her carnival, while not a match for that of Venice or Florence, it was just as lively. The administrators fraternized with the people. The Commandant, it must be said, was not Miragoânais. The police commissioner, General Romulus Joseph, on the other hand, was the town's own son. Miragoâne was proud of Romulus and Romulus would boast about the town. They were made for each other. Also, since Romulus has ceased to exist, Miragoâne is no longer Miragoâne.

I

OF A MEDIUM HEIGHT, his lean body of the most handsome black, Romulus carried his fifty-eight years cheerfully. The rugged severity of his face, decorated with a short moustache and a tuft of silver on his chin, demanded respect. No one in town could remember an instance when Romulus had been treated with anything less than reverence. The testimony of sons concurred with that of their fathers. A man of duty, even if he was ostensibly married to two women—the first, Virginia, a mulatta with silky hair and sumptuous skin, had given him eleven children, all still living; the other, Isménie, an attractive negress with sparkling eyes and sensual lips, had given him thirteen, all equally full of life—if, then, he was ostensibly married to two women, at least he did not appear to show preference and stayed indifferently at the home of one or the other, and neither Virginia nor Isménie resented the other.

Isménie lived in the Detour and Virginia lived on the Islet. Upon their birth, Romulus recognized all of the children as his own, and a member of the Miragoâne Elite had held them on the baptismal fount. It was thus that every inhabitant of the Miragoâne area was either a blood relative of Romulus' or a godparent to one of his children. And for someone like Romulus, a godparent is more than a parent.

There is only enough space to speak of Romulus' elder sons: Pétion, Christophe, Boyer, Toussaint and Rothschild. His mulatta wife had given him Christophe and Toussaint, and from his black wife: Pétion, Boyer and Rothschild. By thus aligning the often-adversarial national colours with Jewish finance, Romulus considered himself to have proved his political sagacity to the nation. That attitude didn't hurt anyone. Pétion, the eldest, was a carpenter. He made an honourable living in the town of Jérémie; Christophe was a cargo manager on board the schooner *God Protects*, which belonged to a merchant named Etienne Trévier. Toussaint, another brother, was Mr. Trévier's assistant. Toussaint considered himself high society. On the first day of the year he would unfailingly send a business card to all of the town's notables, "with his condolences for the loss of another good year." And don't think he was joking. Toussaint Romulus Joseph never joked. And Boyer, he never did anything. He waited. No one ever knew what he was waiting for.

As for Rothschild, his vocation was as a hairdresser. He cut the hair of Miragoâne's respectable citizens—or rather, what he considered Miragoâne respectable citizens. Rothschild arbitrarily divided the population into two groups: the "beaux mondes" and the "ruffians." But where did the "ruffians" begin and the "beaux mondes" end? Rothschild took pleasure in fixing the line. Still, it would be nice to see the common men allowing themselves to imagine that Rothschild Romulus Joseph might lower himself to touch their hair with his scissors! In this makeshift and aristocratic barber, there were the instincts of a fierce tyrant, a wild Marat. He spoke of nothing but "killing a few" in order to save the nation. It was while cutting your hair that he would voice his ideas, stopping to give you a pat, calling you by your first name, or "my dear man". Everyone, including his father, thought he might be dangerous. Speaking of the father…

Romulus was in the habit of referring to himself as a "man of letters". By this he meant he knew his letters—he could read. He could also sign his name, and would do so at every occasion, on anything and everything! It was an obsession. Even though he was an illustrious and powerful member of the Lodge of the New City, he found a way to reconcile his 33rd rank with his adherence to the Catholic Church. He never missed a Mass and lived with a fear of God.

The Priest, wanting to take advantage of Romulus' religious disposition, tried to make him commit to the Lord's herd, lost sheep that he was. Romulus happily renounced his membership to Freemasonry and agreed to take his first communion. The priest undertook to catechize him and Romulus seemed to be sincere in his penitence. But they had yet to discuss the matter of his two wives, which the Priest sensed was rather a delicate issue. The Priest brought it up cleverly one month before the religious ceremony.

"Romulus, my friend," said the priest, rolling his *r*s, "you must understand, it is simply not possible to approach the Holy Table in a state of mortal sin."

"Yes father."

"Your life is very irregular, Romulus. The immorality of your conduct is scandalizing more honest souls."

"Yes father."

"And Good Lord does not approve, Romulus. He does not approve, the Good Lord. It was for this reason that, in his infinite goodness, Romulus, He instituted the Holy Sacrament of marriage."

"Yes father."

The priest breathed in and thought to himself: "It's going well. It's going very well."

"So, Romulus, my friend, in order to approach the Holy Table, it is necessary to put an end to this scandal. You must decide to properly marry."

"Yes father."

"And to that end, my friend, it is important that you leave one of those women and marry the other before God and before men."

Romulus reflected for an instant then stood and said to the priest:

"Can't do it father. I love 'em both."

He left the Priest standing there and went "preferring the Muslim life to the Christian one" as the priest said, adding:

"In Africa, while the Arabs conquered thousands of blacks and converted them to Islam, Catholic missions, both Apostolic and Roman, converted less than ten. They are slaves to the flesh. It's dreadful."

Since that event, every time the priest saw Romulus, the following conversation inevitably took place:

"Hello, father."

"Hello, Romulus. You are still living in sin, I presume?"

"Ah! Father, yer askin' too much."

II

ROMULUS' DEFINING CHARACTERISTIC consisted in this: he preferred high society. He was perfectly willing to commit himself against a man from the country, no matter how honest, if the man was in a dispute with a notable from the city—in this way Romulus was the most abject of scoundrels.

But that's how he was and nothing could change him.

It is always a concern when political arrests are part of a town's operation. Romulus always found a way to avoid catching those he was told to arrest.

Never before and never again was there such an unusual police commissioner.

It's true that, until that time, Romulus' functions were never particularly complicated. The town was quiet and no serious orders ever came from Port-au-Prince; Romulus committed his fierce energy to the running of local matters at which he excelled, or so said the experts.

One morning, Mr. Etienne Trévier, one of the town's top merchants, arrived at the Police Station and announced to Romulus that a trunk containing various objects totaling a value of five thousand dollars was stolen from him during the night.

"Five thousand dollars!" said Romulus, jumping to his feet.

"Yes."

"Very well. Your trunk, and all its contents, will be recovered. You may go."

Soon after, Romulus had gathered all of his agents. Adopting his most important-sounding voice, he made the following declaration:

"Last night a trunk containing precious things of a value of five thousand dollars was removed from the home of Mr. Etienne Trévier, a man of high standing in our town. Who goes about after 10 p.m. in Miragoâne? These are not criminals or professional crooks—I've already purged the city of that lot. Who was out last night? It's the police! Would the person who removed the trunk in question—and I know who you are!" he roared, "come and place it under that tree tonight between ten o'clock and midnight. I won't look; I'll stay in my hammock, eyes closed, until midnight. But that trunk had better be under that tree at twelve, or else!"

Early the next morning Romulus called Mr. Trévier back to the Police Station.

"There's your trunk, sir!" he said proudly, pointing to the stolen property, which sat under the nearby tree.

Mr. Trévier was astounded. He checked the contents and confirmed that everything was accounted for.

Romulus shook the merchant's hand excitedly and cried out:

"What do you think of this fine police work?"

"Admirable!" Mr. Trévier said with conviction. "Simply admirable!"

Romulus leaned in close to the merchant.

"And for my part?" he said, narrowing his eyes.

"One hundred dollars," said Mr. Trévier.

"Very good," said Romulus.

For another glimpse of our commissioner in his element, we need only to examine the failed suicide of Ti Bita, the former boatman of the port. Becoming disgusted with life, he had the "carelessness" to hang himself; rescued before it was too late, Ti Bita had to come back to existence. Romulus scolded him severely and then sent him to prison.

"Beat him up but don't kill him," Romulus secretly ordered his agents.

And the whole way there, thanks to several well-placed blows with a *coco macaque* (voodoo walking stick), Ti Bita came to understand how "careless" he had been.

He was locked in a dungeon and his were feet clamped in irons—sure ways to motivate a love for life.

That was how Romulus served the people of his constituency—for their own good.

Because his pay, and the benefits ("bleedings") he got from his citizens, was not enough to support him and his—and you will recall that there were plenty of *his*! —Romulus, along with some local merchants, arranged the custom-free smuggling of some items. "It's good for commerce, our poor little national commerce!" he would say.

Oh! That Romulus, he knew how to sway a person with his political rhetoric. He'd speak of generosity while at the same time working for his own good at the expense of the public. He was quite a modern man.

However, he did have an opponent: the harbourmaster, Coriolan, better known as General Coyo.

Romulus and Coyo were mortal enemies. Their feud was orchestrated by the commandant, who had arranged it right when he took the job.

Coyo spent his time denouncing Romulus, and Romulus strove to overwhelm Coyo. The Commandant enjoyed it: he would listen to each of their complaints and make no decisions. He thought himself to be governing admirably.

Romulus and Coyo were, therefore, mortal enemies. Coyo, always the restless type, wouldn't hear a peep about "djobs" that didn't comply with established duties. Romulus, honest man that he was, was also against such misdeeds, but managed to benefit from the surplus shares, from money that belonged to the nation. Romulus was involved with small "djobs" that operated outside of customs, with undeclared merchandise hidden in the holds of great sailing ships coming in from the United States or Europe, which, with his help, was unloaded on rowboats in the night. Coyo had caught wind of these goings-on and had been keeping his eye on Romulus—but Romulus was aware of Coyo's surveillance.

So Romulus did something very simple.

Every time he had a ship waiting for him in the harbour, full of undeclared merchandise, Romulus found an excuse to get in a quarrel with Coyo and it would inevitably be reported to their authorities in Pont—two leagues from town.

"Coyo, knowing this," you might say, "had only to avoid quarrelling with the commissioner."

As if you think that would be easy for him! Poor old Coyo!

Romulus would show up out of the blue and would pass by the harbourmaster crying:

"Listen up, General Coyo! You're stepping on my toes again!"

"To step on your toes I'd have to be standing."

"'Hafta?' Did you say 'hafta'? You're telling me I 'hafta', are you?"

"But I'm sitting here quietly, and so I'm not…"

"'M'I a liar, then?"

"I didn't say that…"

"You told me "hafta" and then you treated me like a liar! You abuse me in my duties because I'm pointing out your vices. Fine. You're going to pay for it."

And Romulus went straight to the Customs Office and ordered a halt on imports, citing Coyo's brutality.

"Secretary, write the stop order, then bring it to me to sign," the Commandant ordered placidly. He knew exactly what was going on.

The secretary, who went by the tender and rustic name of Myrtil, hastened to write the order in question in her best handwriting, and Coyo, as not to expose himself to the worst conflict, obeyed.

Generally, the next day, merciful Romulus would arrange for the order to be dropped. It's true that in the interval, between eleven at night and three in the morning, the vessel in question was relieved of all its contents. And since the merchants, on Romulus' advice, always took care to offer significant presents to the Commandant at the right moment, he never investigated too deeply, despite the harbourmaster's repeated accusations.

One day Coyo decided to speak openly with the Commandant. He gave a laudable and eloquent plea for the man to open his eyes. But the Commandant was locked into the following reply, as if in a citadel:

"I'm a soldier first. You'll never see me swaying from military discipline. You disrespected General Romulus; he asked that you be punished. I have nothing else to say!"

"But it's a disgraceful mockery..."

"Enough, General Coriolan, enough! Your acts of brutality are so frequent that I'm actually amazed that General Romulus has been so restrained with the punishment he's had me inflict on you. Twenty-four hour stop order! You're right! It is a mockery!"

"General..."

"Enough! You may go! And if I can give you one piece of advice: Walk straight back to your workplace and don't get mixed up in things that don't concern you! You'll be better off! Goodbye!"

"But..."

"Your situation is worse than you think... Besides these repeated acts of brutality, you forget that you're not from the area... You forget that the population doesn't care for you and the District Commander is against you. That's your problem!

I'm the only thing keeping you here, do me a favour and don't make my job harder than it is... You've been warned."

Coyo, with his trained eye, had discovered that various objects were hidden away in the corner of the plaza's Hotel. These had recently been deposited there. There were hams, a bag of rice, two tins of lard and two of butter, a case of smoked herring, a case of Fay Brothers' soap, a case of Bordeaux, and three rolls of fine wool—Coyo heeded the warning of his superior, saying to himself: "leave it."

And from then on, like his boss, he closed his eyes and was better off.

"I'm too good," Romulus said to himself, not without profound satisfaction, caressing his salt-and-pepper goatee.

III

NONETHELESS, THE JOIE DE VIVRE that permeated the town was soon replaced with a deafening melancholy. The reddish limestone of Bel-Air and Morne Blanc seemed to be fading to a greyish hue, and the green and rocky mountain, at the foot of which Miragoâne lay, was visibly paling.

In hushed voices, people were speaking of revolution, of the return of the exiles. Among the exiles were two sons of Miragoâne: Boileau Laforest and Resilius Rincher. The fame of Boileau Laforest was such that in the New City a person in a fit of excitement was said to have a "Boileau look!"

A rural woman, who was passing by carrying a pot of syrup on her head, fell down stone dead. Her name was Cinette.

So sadness and anxiety hovered over the little town. Generals with strange names and funny hats would come and go. Severe and specific instructions would come from Port-au-Prince on how to treat any exiles who showed up in Miragoâne. The uneasiness grew each day. Romulus himself was anxious and sullen. In the streets, you could hear things like: "I'll defend the society against all odds." A messenger showed up with an order for the arrest of Scipionnice Scipio, to be taken dead or alive.

Scipionnice was a goldsmith who lived in the Detour. He was a hardworking and peaceful citizen who had nothing to gain from a revolution.

Each year, he went off into the foothills to sell the feeble little pieces of jewellery he had fashioned during the off-season. He had done nothing to justify being denounced as someone stirring up the masses to revolt.

Scipionnice Scipio was esteemed and loved by the people of Miragôane; they knew he was harmless. Rothschild-Isménie himself—in Miragôane the mother's name is used to distinguish children as legitimate or bastards—Rothschild-*Isménie* himself, the malevolent man par excellence, proclaimed the "correctness" of Scipionnice.

What anguish in Miragôane the morning of his arrest!

As the townsmen smoked their after-coffee cigarettes—the best ones! —they saw Romulus passing by at dawn—first one way and then the other. He was in "semi" which is to say he had "broken out" his red vest and his large blue tunic with the gold buttons—standard fare for the division general—while he had kept his brown bourgeois cap and his even more bourgeois twill trousers.

Romulus' extreme austerity, enhanced by his famous blue glasses, which were like a war decoration to him, was enough to chill the soul.

Soon he passed by once more, followed by five police agents armed with muskets.

Arriving on the Islet, he yelled: "Halt!" at his house. Then he went in to Virginia, asked for some grog, and slipped her the following words:

"Go tell Scipionnice to hide in the woods."

After which, having ingested his shot of absinthe, Romulus returned to the Police Station in the New City, added five men to his police squad and went on to the Detour to apprehend "that troublesome Scipionnice—dead or alive," as he uttered every ten seconds.

When they got to Scipionnice's door Romulus again shouted: "Halt!" Convinced without a doubt that the instruction he had given his wife would have been too late, he began fiercely barking orders. To give Scipionnice one last chance he fired his revolver in the air twice, and then the house was surrounded. Addressing deputy commissioner Choute, Romulus roared:

"Commissioner, take five men with you, go in and take that public enemy dead or alive."

Choute, followed by five agents, broke into the house and came back out, dejected, two minutes later. Romulus' face brightened.

"Gen'ral," said Choute, "the house is empty."

"By thunder!" Romulus yelled. "You let the bird fly free! Sirs," he added to the police agents. "Sirs, take deputy commissioner Choute to prison! Clap him in irons! Make sure both his feet are bound in iron."

"But gen'ral..."

"Go! And be sure to follow my orders quickly!"

Two hours later, when it was established that Scipionnice wasn't in his house at the time that Choute broke in, the Commandant ordered Choute to be released.

This affair would have consequences.

President Salomon blamed the District Commander who blamed the Commandant who blamed Romulus who blamed Choute who blamed the five officers. They couldn't find anyone to blame, and so consoled themselves by killing a countryman, beating him to death with a *coco macaque.* He had been accused of stealing a turkey.

But the chain of blame wasn't the only consequence. After an in-depth investigation comprised of various formal and informal reports of this memorable arrest, President Salomon decided simply to fire Romulus. The two shots the commissioner had fired, despite his colourful explanations, were deemed highly unorthodox—so the president named a new police commissioner for Miragoâne. This was General Locean Daphnis or Daphnis Locean (no one ever knew which).

...But it didn't matter
If Locean was the former or Daphnis the latter.

It mattered even less that, on arriving in the town, the Lepine Brothers named him Chirepite—and no one would call him anything else. The nickname suited him perfectly.

It must be said that the Commandant, Choute and the other deputy commissioner were also replaced—even though the latter had nothing to do with it.

A few days after the installation of these new officers, Miragoâne woke to an appalling panic. At the market, in the streets and under the galleries, people spoke in hushed voices, remarks that would shock any stranger—the type of remarks that must have circulated under the Roman Republic: "Brutus stayed home—and Scipio? I heard he was taken in? —Never! —Seems that Sulla is on the run! —But Sulla is a nobody— Nobody's a nobody; everyone's a suspect—There's no reason for this to be happening—Someone implicated Cicero—No! — Yes, Caesar Octavian has arrested him."

Elsewhere in the town, it seemed like you'd been transported to Athens, on the Pnyx or in the Agora: "And Demosthenes? —He wasn't worried; such a quiet man—That's fair—But Aristides was arrested under Mrs. Euripides' gallery —Oh, the poor devil! —Yes, it was Aristomenes that took him."

In reality, Chirepite, with the help of the two new deputy commissioners, had taken in a quarter of the male population of the town. And though Romulus himself hadn't been bothered, at least two of his sons (Toussiant-Virginia and Boyer-Isménie) found themselves among the political prisoners. The following Sunday, they were all loaded on the sloop *Equality* and shipped off to Port-au-Prince where they were shut up in the dungeons of the Centre Street Palace.

Miragoâne fell into a profound torpor.

IV

INTO A PROFOUND TORPOR, MIRAGOÂNE HAD FALLEN—and Romulus went with it. It was always a sinister ordeal, being locked in the Port-au-Prince Palace dungeon. But this particular time, at the start of 1883, the ordeal was more than sinister—it was deadly.

Ten months earlier, twenty-eight well-known citizens, after having withstood the dungeon, the secrecy and the irons, were judged and condemned to death by a special military council. Fourteen were executed on 5 May in Saint-Marc and fourteen on 6 May in Gonaïves. Among the dead were Mathurin Lys, Mentor Nicolas, Maurille Lafontant, Théophile Parisien, Georges Haentgens, Mesinin Alexis, O'Brien Jr. and Prosper Bellanton.

Other citizens were in prison, still others on the run: "Whoever isn't with me is against me!" was the declaration of the new Restorer. Since Dessalines, people had kept trying to restore this poor country, a country that only wanted one thing: to be left in peace. But how could it be when people came up to you and said plainly: "Brother, join me, bow down to me, or die!"

17

And so terror hovered over the Republic and dread filled the people. Even so, in Miragoâne one man was calm: Romulus. With his silence, he protested against the deplorable state of things. Besides the merchant, Etienne Trévier, Romulus was never seen talking with anyone but the Manager of Financial Administration, Mr. Octavius Merlin. Merlin was a liberal Bazelaisist, though an officer of the State commissioned by President Salomon.

Formerly top of his class at Port-au-Prince Secondary School, Octavius Merlin was the pride of Miragoâne. He had ascribed himself a sort of moral function consisting of distributing intellectual pleasures to the general population. They were grateful for this. Suave, smooth and charming, his personality was consolation for his soul, which overflowed with idealism. At the end of every year, he more or less successfully arranged to have the young people of the town perform a few plays, free for all to see. He was at once the director, principal actor and orchestra conductor. He nearly died, so to speak, to get the thing done; but wasn't it worth it for the sake of art? And then, he couldn't break the tradition. As a child he had seen *Le Cid* performed in front of an enthralled Miragoâne. And what actors! Mr. Constant Gentil played the role of Rodrigo and Mr. Saint-Macary Fauché, that of Don Diego. As for Chimene, a delectable young woman had the part: Miss Victorine Mauclerc—who can still be seen today, an obscure virgin dragging her remains about the blinding streets of Port-au-Prince, alas! *Sic transit...*

Thus, Octavius Merlin was the pride of Miragoâne and for that reason Romulus loved him. But since the young man was so arrogant their relationship grew only gradually.

Nevertheless, it grew.

One day, back when he was the commissioner, Romulus showed up "in person" at the Financial Administration Office to lodge a complaint about the Police "documentation." Merlin, undoubtedly absorbed in his literary preoccupations, didn't remember the police commissioner's name, and attempting not to hurt his feelings, responded to his cordial greeting with this metaphor:

"Hey! Well, *old tiger*," he said, "how are you doing, sir?"

Romulus beamed as if he had caught a glimpse of paradise. To be called *old tiger*, which is to say, valiant, brave and heroic, by such an intelligent young man... how sweet!

After that, Romulus and Merlin became friends and it could be said that the link that united them has only grew stronger.

In the sombre hours in March of 1883 Merlin was the only being with whom Romulus exchanged *political ideas*—and the ideas that Merlin passed on to the former commissioner would prove to be fatal for the latter.

Merlin's mind had been tainted by the sentimentalism of the *History of the Girondists* and the risky false philosophy of Victor Hugo's later years. He was sensitive to oration, and by consequence devoid of all critical sense. A passionate attendee of the House debates of 1876, he was quickly converted to Bazelaisism. Boyer Bazelais, after having declared at the top of the forum that he had almost reached a point of absolute perfection, felt obliged to carry his liberalism from the discussion at hand to the seizure of the power by armed coup. Merlin was convinced without giving a second thought; he calmly prepared himself for an insurrection. And like the Greek child from Hugo's *Les Orientales*, he might have written:

Give me powder and bullets.

And naturally, poor Romulus wanted them too. After that Romulus could be heard speaking of tyranny, of oppression and liberty!

V

IT WAS UNDER THE GALLERY of the merchant Etienne Trévier, on a Sunday morning, that Octavius Merlin, always endorsed by Romulus, unburdened himself by exposing his dreams for the future.

Mr. Trévier lived near the garrison, which was (and still is) also the market on the seaside of Miragoâne. A "memorial fountain" in the laneway, inaugurated sometime earlier by President Salomon, was the only decoration in the plaza. Anchored only a few steps away, foreign brigs with their masts and ropes constituted an integral part of the décor. Attached to the land with simple planks, these great sailing ships were continuously replaced: arriving full of merchandise, they soon left again loaded up with logwood.

Octavius Merlin, Romulus and Mr. Trévier were talking together, this Sunday 25 March, 1883 while watching the well-dressed women pass by. These women, in their lilac shawls and Indian headscarves, in their leafy-patterned fabric and feathered caps, were strutting through the plaza on their way to Mass.

The conversation, which had petered off a number of times as each man had much on his mind, was revived when Octavius Merlin, with an irritated expression, said in a low voice:

"A country like Haiti, which, as we all know, is famous for its great parliamentary battles, can no longer, must no longer be under the control of Salomon."

"Who do we have to thank for Salomon," replied Mr. Trévier, "if not your Boyer Bazelais? Because the logical process of things should have ruled out the former Minister of Soulouque…"

"You're kidding!" Merlin interrupted naïvely. "It's Boisrond-Canal that we have to thank for Salomon. If Boisrond had simply surrendered his power to Bazelais, the obvious choice…"

Mr. Trévier shrugged his shoulders and continued:

"It was Boyer Bazelais who, by his insurrection of 30 June, disrupted the natural order and succession of events. The virtually unknown Salomon, seeing his chance to profit, took the power that was laid before him thanks to the unwitting efforts of the Haitian liberal leader, Boyer Bazelais, who, as you know well my dear Octavius, is an authoritative liberal— two words that scream discordance when placed next to each other. It's been said, in any case, that the insurgent never knows what the outcome of his deeds will be, but, by taking action, he 'creates movements, currents, disrupts order and makes cracks in the foundation of the State which would have stayed dormant without this shock.' And that is why we have Boyer Bazelais to thank for Salomon, even though on the surface it seems paradoxical."

Merlin responded to this argument with a slew of curses about the powers that be—all the while in an extremely hushed voice.

"For my part," said Etienne Trévier, "Mr. Salomon might be all that you say he is; I don't care. I choose to have nothing to do with the government, and I hope they treat me likewise. I'm as shocked as anyone by arbitrary atrocities. But since I can't do anything about it, I have no choice but to move on and stick to my own affairs—I have my son to raise and a wife and an old mother who have no one on earth but me to support them. You understand that I'd be a wretch if I abandoned my business and my schooner, which allow me independence, to occupy myself with what doesn't concern me, in sum."

"The situation in this country," said Merlin, "requires all good men to rise up as one to overthrow an abhorrent government."

"It goes without saying," Romulus agreed.

"Here, at least, is a serious man," said Merlin, shaking the hand of the former police commissioner.

"Don't worry yourself with the government, my dear Octavius," Etienne Trévier resumed. "Follow the good example that old Papa Merlin gave his whole life: work for your own interests. I didn't like your father much; in fact I have an unpleasant memory of him, since he was an evil old man. One day when I was busy filling out a ledger after some transactions, there, close to Mitchell's place, your father snuck up on me like a wolf and jammed his bony fingers in my eyes."

The other two men laughed with delight and Mr. Trévier added:

"Who, in Miragoâne, had never been a victim of the evil deeds of Saint-Just Merlin? He did as he pleased! I remember a certain blow to the head of our friend Romulus, a certain day when Romulus, with no ill intent, was dozing against Virginia's house."

"That's the truth, it is," said Romulus, regaining his composure. "But, since it was Papa Saint-Just, we didn't do anything about it."

"Still," resumed Mr. Trévier, "he was a hard worker. He should be imitated in that respect, Octavius. Every afternoon a great quantity of logwood arrives in the New City. Restore the scale that your father had built there, Octavius. Buy wood on credit from the merchants in the plaza (for my part, I'm inclined to advance you any funds you may need). That will be more profitable than trying to change things that never change —an unworthy task for such an individual! —and it will be more worth your time than whatever the *Œil* says, whatever Bazelais thinks and whatever Salomon ruminates. Almost a century of civil wars," Mr. Trévier added, "has shown us that if the Haitian political regime isn't in line with the views of a particular faction, the best move is to let the regime follow its due course while the progressive faction continues developing through business, becoming stronger as absolutism thrashes in vain. In that way, gradually, we'll see political power move to the middle class for the benefit of everyone. It is already happening in many civilized nations."

"My dear sir," Romulus said in a profound tone, "Haiti's a black man's country, and a black man's country is not a white man's country. When a government's not good, you hafta overthrow it and replace it with a good government, m'I right, Octavius?"

"You're words are golden, my dear Romulus," Merlin replied passionately. "You speak at once with good sense and with patriotism. Etienne thinks of nothing but his own selfish interests—his money, his wife and his son. He never bothers to reach out to his dying fatherland..."

"Another tall tale!" Mr. Trévier said. "In what way is Haiti dying?"

"Speak softer, my friend," Romulus whispered, afraid.

"Has this country ever been more prosperous?" Mr. Trévier continued quietly. "The coffee harvest was superb this year, almost five million pounds more than last year, and shipped coffee costs 7 piasters 50 centimes currently, and in Le Havre it's valued at 60 francs. The exchange rate was 15% at the start of this month and has fallen to 10% according to the latest news from Port-au-Prince; and even though it's only March, here in Miragoâne we've already surpassed last year's imports and exports by far. And there's reason to believe it's the same all over the country."

Merlin took Etienne Trévier's arm:

"But this government... this government!"

"But this government is a natural product of its environment, and not, therefore, its cause," said Mr. Trévier. "The cause, or rather the causes, of our social maladies are ignorance and isolation. To fight this malady we must train up individuals—we must above all make sure not to needlessly annihilate the individuals we already have in the kind of bloody adventure you are proposing. Furthermore, and this is

25

important, Octavius, there will never be a prestigious government in Haiti, because we know them too well."

Merlin stood up and said:

"Quite obviously, my friend, you are for Salomon. I always assumed your sympathies lay with Bazelais, who is the epitome of honour…"

"I repeat," Mr. Trévier interrupted, "that I'm not a political man, and so I'm not for this one or that one. My interests, and fifteen years of hard work, have made me an anti-revolutionary. I have more than one million pounds of logwood piled up in the New City, nine hundred bags of coffee ready to be shipped, not to mention my two halls that each contain thirty thousand dollars' worth of merchandise—all paid for with my logwood and my coffee! You can see why a civil war wouldn't be to my benefit. Miragoâne is the most likely city in the Republic for the exiles to return to. If that happens it'll be my ruin, the destruction of all my hard work—the best thing, perhaps, that our town has ever accomplished."

"That's the truth," said Romulus.

"You won't be ruined, Etienne," Merlin said with enthusiasm. "As soon as Bazelais takes power he'll make up for all your losses."

"Come on!" Mr. Trévier exclaimed. "He would have enough to deal with for the compensation owed to foreigners! — Besides, he won't take power. He is indeed a man of great ability and patriotism in the highest degree. I just don't think his discernment is at the same level. His idealism will be his demise. Counting on the enthusiasm of the Haitian people is like counting on the void. A people with their origin in slavery are a nonexistent people, if I dare say such a thing. Furthermore, there's never been a revolution by the people of Haiti like there has in France, notably in 1830 and 1848."

Merlin smiled with pity.

"And the War of Independence," he said, "who carried that out? And the revolution of 1843 and all the ones that followed?"

"The War of Independence," Mister Trévier replied, "was essentially a military coup. It was by terrorizing the field-workers and shooting the hesitant that Dessalines was able to raise the masses against the whites. And what masses! Of the thirty thousand combatants, there were twenty thousand soldiers and only ten thousand armed farmers. That's what Dessalines, after all his hard work, was able to raise: ten thousand men out of a total population of five hundred thousand inhabitants in 1803! —The revolution of 1843 was similarly carried out by the military, at the behest of the bourgeois who were only really interested in military decorations though they ranted about the principles of liberty. The other Haitian revolutions are all the same; the pikes are raised with the army behind them."

Romulus showed his approval by smugly hitting his chest with his fist.

"Without the military, nothing can be done," Romulus said.

"And that makes sense," Mr. Trévier continued, "because it's the only organized force in the country—it's a dead weight to be sure, but it's a weight."

"If things are as you say," Merlin replied, "then there's nothing left to do but to throw up our arms in despair. Well, or to fold under the yoke of the military or resolve to emigrate."

"There's a third option," said Mr. Trévier, "and it's the best one; we must build a social class strong enough that the powers will be forced to account for it. I ask you to observe that this class is in the process of forming: it is Haitian commerce. A new civil war would be its death, since the tendency of the government is to annihilate this class because the sympathies of those in Haitian commerce are mostly with Bazelais. Therefore, I fear an act of Bazelais as I fear a catastrophe. In the same way that Gambetta preferred to relinquish power rather than govern with his friends, if he was successful, Bazelais might stay in power, but he would unable to effectively organize anything, because his efforts would be paralyzed by his friends—against whom he couldn't do anything since he would owe them everything. With Bazelais vanquished, this country would backslide horribly. And this is what we'd see: Haitians who had previously achieved a respectable position, and who were then ruined by the war, would not only ask the State for their subsistence, but each would try to make his fortune at the expense of the community. There would be no more Haitian commerce, no more administrative control, no more political debate. Everyone would be an official or a dependant. We would be a people of dependants on the State—a State without glory, without credit and without money. And the crown of this beautiful edifice would be shameless denunciation, shameless prostitution and shameless begging."

"Oh! Etienne!" Merlin cried, twisting his hands. "What sinister predictions! Luckily you're exaggerating! The important thing is that we rid the country of a harmful system that outrages the European continent."

"Don't worry," Mr. Trévier replied, "the system will last for a long time still; it is adequate for the Haitian temperament, in the sense that all good Haitians have but one objective: privilege for himself and oppression for others, and the system provides exactly that."

"And Europe!" cried Merlin. "And Europe which has its eyes fixed on us!"

"If you sincerely believe what you're saying," said Mr. Trévier sadly, "then you are fit to be pitied, Octavius."

At that moment, Mrs. Trévier, who was coming home from Mass with her son, arrived on the porch. With a gracious smile the young woman shook the hands of Romulus and Merlin, and then greeted her husband with an affectionate gesture. Mr. Trévier, all the while patting the child's cheeks, asked his wife the same thing he did every Sunday:

"How was the Mass today?"

"Lovely," Mrs. Trévier replied.

"What did Father le Marguer talk about?"

"About the gossip that is dividing the town. He said lots of disagreeable things to the faithful."

"As usual then," Mr. Trévier laughed.

Addressing Romulus, Mrs. Trévier added:

"I haven't seen you at High Mass for some time. Have you become a miscreant like Mr. Merlin?"

"Oh! Not at all Mrs. Etienne!" Romulus said, ashamed. "I regularly go to Low Mass. I believe in God."

"When it's convenient!"

And Mrs. Trévier quietly disappeared into the hallway of her house. The doors below were closed since the ground floor of the house was a "finery" shop operated by Mrs. Trévier.

"Off you go Paul," said Mr. Trévier, "hurry up and go see your grandma."

The child waved to the group and headed off in the direction of the Seaside Road.

Twenty minutes later he returned to find Mr. Trévier in the dining room with Romulus and Merlin. They were in the process of savouring a cocktail of dark rum—darker still, since Romulus had insisted on having two fingers of tafia added to his, to take off the "*big heat there*", as he explained it to Mrs. Trévier.

Around ten o'clock, Romulus and Merlin left. Mr. Trévier spent the rest of the morning reading *Revue des deux Mondes*. That afternoon, the merchant went on horseback to pay a little visit to his logwood piled up in the New City.

VI

MR. TRÉVIER'S ROOM faced the plaza. On Monday night he thought he heard a scratchy voice yelling his father's name: "Almonacy! Almonacy!" Mr. Trévier woke with a start, listened carefully and realized that a murmur was coming both from the Seaside and Main Street. "Bah!" he said to himself, "some military exercise, no doubt." And remembering that the District Commander and a government delegation had been in Miragoâne for the past few days, he added: "to take defensive precautions." He fell back into a profound sleep. Around six o'clock in the morning, two quick knocks on the door woke him up again.

Mrs. Trévier donned a robe and left the room; soon she returned and woke her husband, saying: "It's Romulus."

"Tell him to come up," he said, getting dressed and guessing that something was seriously wrong.

He knew he was right as soon as he saw how Romulus was dressed.

With a sixteen calibre in his hand, a cuff on his side, his belt decked with bullets and his neck wrapped in a red handkerchief, Romulus said in a martial manner:

"The Gen'ral-in-Chief is asking for you."

"Which General-in-Chief?"

"General Boyer Bazelais."

"You must be kidding!"

Romulus opened the balcony door and said: "Look!"

Mr. Trévier looked out on the plaza and saw, in the grey morning, armed men all dressed the same in short, blue denim tunics billowing over their fancy cloth trousers, all wearing black felt caps. It was the exiles.

Mr. Trévier went pail and murmured:

"They didn't meet resistance?"

"No. The bulk of the exiles landed at Saint-Romme and then divided into three columns under the general command of Boyer Bazelais and conducted by Désorme Gresseau, Brutus Casimir and Boileau Laforest who marched onto the District Office by way of the Spanish Fountain. When they got to Fort Malet some guns were fired into the air; hearing these, the District Commander and the Commandant, as well as the government delegation, fled without looking back. This morning some plumes were found on the ground on Main Street. The District Commander went to Ahrendts. The exiles immediately occupied the District Office and fired more gunshots into the air. This signaled their boat, the *Tropic*, to anchor in the harbour, and for the remaining exiles to disembark, complete with two howitzer cannons and cases of munitions. And there you have it."

Mr. Trévier replied:

"Around four o'clock, someone going by on horseback was calling my father's name."

"That was Boileau. I heard it too before he came to get me. He hadn't heard of your father's death. I told him the news. He asked me to go fetch you... Around five thirty he took me to the General-in-Chief. He introduced me to him, slapping me on the shoulder and saying: "Here's a man for you, *this boy*!" Boyer took my hand in his and *chatted with me*. He is a very *good man*, Etienne; I'm ready to give my very life for him, *my very life*... Now," Romulus added, "I have to leave you; I'm being sent on a mission to contact a man called Cléovil Modé with three of the exiles. Don't waste a second; they're waiting for you at the headquarters."

And with these last words Romulus left.

Left alone, Mr. Trévier paced back and forth in his room anxiously snapping his fingers. Then he abruptly cried out:

"What the devil do they want with me?"

At that moment, Octavius Merlin, armed to the teeth, burst into the room.

"I don't mean you any harm, Etienne," he said. "The Chief of Operations wants to meet with you, as with one of the town nobility, that's all. I was sent here to make sure you got the message from Romulus."

Mr. Trévier put on his hat and cried:

"All right, I'm going."

He headed down the stairs. Merlin followed him. The stairway led to the dining room. There he met a handsome exile with a lush black beard. The exile introduced himself:

"Mr. Perpignand of Port-au-Prince," he said.

"A pleasure, sir."

"Your wife was kind enough to offer me a cup of coffee... what a delight our country's coffee is! And what a joy to be back in the fatherland!"

"The fact is," Mr. Trévier groaned, "that you entered a bit suddenly."

"Yes... We've come to overthrow this Mr. Salomon's government," the exile added, doing the most pleasant pirouette in the world—a pirouette that landed him near the table so he could set down his empty cup.

"Excuse me, sir," he added, "but the fleeing authorities might return with reinforcements to retake the town that we've seized as a base of operations... But it's not only Miragoâne that we've taken; this very morning we're emissaries to the principal authorities of the South Province and the District of Jacmel. Before long, therefore, we'll advance on Port-au-Prince. In the meantime, sir, I am unfortunately obliged to leave your comfortable home to go and see my friend Epaminondas Desroches, to give him a hand building the barricade at the Detour, of which he is in charge. Good bye."

"Take care."

In the boutique, Mr. Trévier found his wife who was very busy selling shoes to a large group of exiles who had had to walk in the water after a faulty boat-landing operation. Mrs. Trévier was a Lambert, of Jérémie. One of the exiles, Samuel Blanchet, who was from the same city, had brought his companions to her with the laudable sentiment of Jérémians that makes them seek each other out, as if they were a single large and close-knit family.

34

Mrs. Trévier introduced her husband to her clients as if she had known them for ten years.

"Etienne, this is Mr. Duperrier Cazeau."

"Of Jacmel, sir!"

"Pleased to meet you, sir."

"Mr. Bethard the Younger."

"Ah! The tribune—a pleasure, sir."

"Mr. Albert Elie—Mr. Gaston Elie—Mr. Alphonse Barthole —Mr. Dantès Matnon—Mr. Constantine Rigaud—Mr. Jules Arbuthnot—Mr. Lys—Mr. Alexandre David—Mr. Bélomon Duvivier—Mr. Charles Bazelais—Mr. Roy—Mr. Charles Geffrard—Mr. Warlock Déjoie."

The handshakes multiplied.

"Etienne, here is General Désormes Gresseau!"

"Ah! Ah…"

When the first ones left others appeared to replace them; they were brilliant minds, like Franck Solages and Succés Bigaille; gentlemen, like Talleyrand and Toussaint Laroche; remarkably well-known blacks, like Ulysses Fourreau, Etienne and Henry Supplice, Arécius Rénélique… To the last few, Mr. Trévier said:

"Please excuse me, sirs, for not staying with you longer, but your leader is expecting me."

"Ah! Very good… very good."

And, accompanied by Merlin, Mr. Trévier went from under the gallery. The *Tropic* had weighed anchor and left. The sun shone cheerfully on the garrison, which was animated with the coming and going of the exiles. They were: Brave and Alexis Béliard, Loctamar Mayard, Mathurin Legros, Lucéna Léveillé,

O'Brien, Moulite Taffet, Valery Sterlin, Prévost Chavannes, Luc Elie, Planchet Audigé, Charles Lassègue, Charles Mathurin, Edouard Buthler, Geffrard Lucas, Aimé Legros Jr., Alexis Plésance, Blain (of Cap-Hatien) and his son-in-law Dantès Martin, Pio Rigaud (of Saint-Marc) and his two sons Turenne and William. And all of them, young and old, were cheerful, lively, and full of spirit. The young men of Miragoâne, the sons of Porrcely Vigué, Spirius Lorquet, Morel Jacob, Constant Lolague, Rousselin Montpérous, Elie Derenoncour, Oméra and Dupuytren Arnoux and fifty others, all happy with their lives of action, mingled enthusiastically with the rest.

Mr. Trévier, still accompanied by Merlin, was crossing the plaza diagonally and heading toward the north side of Main Street when a drummer, followed by some soldiers, halted nearby and drew the attention of the crowd with his rolling sound.

It was a "pronouncement." Mr. Trévier stopped and a dozen townspeople flocked to the spot. An old black exile, wearing a flat-sided hat, started to shout a *Decree*, by which the *Central Revolutionary Committee* declared President Salomon deposed from his high post of First Magistrate of the Republic. And the old black exile, every time that he encountered President Salomon's name on his paper, howled: "that fat pig!"

When this orator, who was a bit dull and whose name was Clavius Claude, arrived at the names of the members of the Committee, signers of this proclamation, Mr. Trévier was more than a little surprised to hear his own name among the others.

"They've gone too far," he said, continuing down Main Street.

"It was Boileau," Merlin said excitedly, "it was Boileau that added your name, as your representative."

"I sympathize with him," Mr. Trévier replied, "but I can't accept that."

"Just wait, Etienne, just wait and see. Don't get carried away."

"I'm not carried away. I've never been calmer," Mr. Trévier said coldly.

While they were talking, the two men arrived outside of the District Office, which had been made into the revolutionary headquarters. They found themselves between two groups of exiles, among whom they recognized reputable men, such as Brutus Casimir, the former senator, who held the platonic title of "Chief Commander of Revolutionary Forces." Also present were Gélus Bienaimé, Magnan, Joseph Muller, Adolphe Pinchinat the Elder, Diogenes Bras; and other younger men like Jean-Baptiste Ramir Chenet, Massillon Jean-Bart, Bouraine Sr., Auguste Kavanagh, Hannibal Beaugé, Vilmar Péan, Robert Jean Pierre, Paul Etienne, Turenne Guerrier, Lascases Samson, Stanislas Bariento, Antonin Boncy, Moreau the Younger, Jean-Pierre Bazelais, Alfred Brisard, Joachim Nicolas, Thermitus Rosier, Antoine Nicolas, Vincent-Guerrier Loiseau, Titon and Adamar Passé (of Saint-Marc), Pinchinat the Younger, Modés, Godefroy Noël, Resilius Rincher, Charles Desroches, Philoxenus Bazin (who was the son-in-law of Désormes Gresseau), Paulémon Berthaud (the brother of the tribune)…

It seemed to Mr. Trévier that some of them were complaining about the sudden departure of the American vessel the *Tropic*, which was supposed to have stayed at their disposal for three months.

"Certainly," a young exile insisted, "Bazelais suggested that this would happen."

"Wait for me here," Merlin said to Mr. Trévier as he headed into the crowed Office. "I'll be back soon."

"Hey! In front!" a voice cried from behind Mr. Trévier. This was intended to clear the way for three cavalrymen, who appeared utterly romantic in their sombre outer robes and black felt caps with bicolour cockades on one side. Mr. Trévier immediately recognized Duperrier Cazeau among them by his unforgettable brown complexion; he was full of youth, energy and beauty. Another cavalryman, dressed in military tunic with gold buttons, who was known well by Mr. Trévier, joined the other three. This was our friend Romulus.

"Etienne, *adios*!" the former commissioner cried.

"Bon voyage!" Mr. Trévier replied.

And the four horsemen took off at a gallop up Main Street, reached the New City and disappeared from view.

The group of exiles resumed chatting in the street beneath the gallery when out of the District Office came a tall and lean man with a red handkerchief around his neck and a Panama hat on his head. He crossed the gallery and hurried toward Etienne with open arms.

"Kiss me, my little man!"

And Boileau Laforest—since it was he! —pasted his toothless mouth against that of Etienne Trévier under the

38

compassionate and approving gaze of Merlin, who had followed his General out of the building. After introducing the Miragoânais merchant to his friends, Boileau said to him:

"Come, my little man, come with me."

He took Mr. Trévier into the house where the Chief of Operations was staying. Boileau went alone into a room where he talked in a hushed voice with someone. He then came back out and told the merchant he could enter.

A few seconds later, Mr. Trévier found himself face-to-face with a man of slightly less than average height in a dark green military habit and white trousers. It was Boyer Bazelais.

He quietly welcomed Mr. Trévier, and in a kind, affectionate tone invited the merchant to sit with him.

In very clear language, the Chief of Operations laid out the goal of his expedition, which was to establish a new regime following the principles of the Constitution of 1867; he said that the revolution was arranged in such a way that it was sure to succeed; that the landing of the exiles in Miragoâne was sure to evoke an extraordinary commotion throughout the nation; that the Revolution would spread like wildfire from one end of the Republic to the other. As for organization, he said that committees should be composed of local leaders; that these committees, when the Revolution was complete, would have to appoint a proportional number of their members as delegates; that these delegates would unite in a general assembly to form a provisional government which would manage the country until elections could be held for a new Head of State. That was why Mr. Etienne Trévier was chosen, to be a part of the committee, as a part of the Miragoâne elite.

"I regret that I am unable to accept," said Mr. Trévier.

"Might I ask why?"

"Because I've long since decided not to be involved in politics. I'm an anti-revolutionary to the core of my being."

So the Chief of Operations began to explain the country's political situation in great detail, explaining that the current absolutism, being a reign of personal rule, could only be contrary to the benefit of the people. People only develop under the force of liberalism, of which the essence is control; finally, he concluded by explaining the need for men of merit to be involved with public affairs, since absolutism in politics is something so horrid that Haiti was honour bound to rid themselves of it. He added that the individual merit of each Haitian is representative of their entire race.

"So you must join us," he advised.

Mr. Trévier listened to this heated, colourful, nuanced discourse. The sincerity was touching. In this pale man, with his broad forehead and prophet-worthy beard, he sensed immense pride—and though, as everyone knows, vanity is a foolish vice, the pride that a man of virtue feels for his own valour is a very excellent quality. The proud will sacrifice their wealth and their lives for what they believe is right—unlike the vain, who only speak highly of themselves without a solid foundation.

"So Mr. Trévier, can we count on you?"

"It's impossible. I feel a profound sympathy for you and for your ideas; I can tell that you have a good heart and a great soul, which is why I would have liked to be able to help you. I admire and respect you, but not enough to throw myself into a revolution. And your operation will cost me such a disastrous consequence if it fails that I shudder just to think of the moral responsibility that weighs on you."

The revolutionary leader was silent for a moment. Then in a calm voice, carefully shaping each of his words, he said:

"There are those that make revolutions and there are those that provoke them—the guilty ones are the latter. I was forced into the position of an insurgent by the abominable way that the elections were distorted by my rivals…"

"Alas!" said Mr. Trévier. "It's the sad truth of life that human affairs must always be mixed with bad seeds. It's better to accept what has happened—to maintain your liberalism in discussion in the proper venue, in the newspapers and in books —than to end up where you are. If the liberal party is destroyed in the battle that you're trying to fight with a handgun it will be the end of the political balance in our nation. Only the national party will be left standing with no adversaries with whom to debate. It will thus stop developing and break up into deluded cliques looking for power to satisfy their appetites and not to achieve ideals. You can see that even the question of progress in Haiti is currently at stake."

"You're right," Bazelais said with concern, as if speaking to himself. "In fact, I resisted a good deal before initiating this expedition. Apart from Paul, Price and one or two of my other friends who were against it, all these other men pressured me. One day, Talleyrand said: 'Ah! If it was Brice…' the word stung me like whip…"

Realizing that he had become lost in his thoughts, he collected himself and said:

"But I will be triumphant, because…"

"Because…"

"Because Providence will not abandon me."

"Provi…" said Mr. Trévier, as if he had misheard.

"Providence," repeated Bazelais with confidence.

Mr. Trévier rose and expressed the desire to leave.

The revolutionary leader said:

"So you refuse to join my cause?"

"Yes."

"Then, goodbye, sir."

"Good luck, General."

The two men parted, each a bit irritated with the other, but still respectful.

When he got back to his house Mr. Trévier had a hushed conversation with his wife, then after dinner he went up to his room. He came back down later with a large suitcase. He called for his son.

After much searching, Paulémon was found on the Islet, at the spot where the Laroche brothers had started to put up a barricade, and brought back home.

Mr. Trévier scolded his son in a low voice and then kissed him tenderly. He then kissed his wife.

An instant later, he could be seen, suitcase in hand, heading north across the plaza. He arrived in front of the house of the American, Mitchell, on top of which the starry flag waved. He went in.

Mr. Etienne Trévier had gone to the consulate.

VII

ROMULUS HAD LEFT ON HORSEBACK the same morning that the gentlemen had arrived. Accompanied by three Jacmelian exiles —Duperrier Cazeau, Kenscoff Sr. and Vicière Chanlatte—he had been sent on a mission to see a certain Cléovil Modé, of the Iron Coast. The emissaries must not have had far to go; they returned before too long. This Cléovil Modé was the man that Bazelais seemed to count on most. Chanlatte, who claimed to know the man, had led them to "Creek's Crossroads"—the intersection of the road to Aquin Bridge and the mountain path to Jacmel, where he thought he could contact him. Surely, when he heard of the return of the exiles and the impending battle at Miragoâne, Cléovil Modé would be so impressed that he would return at the head of the party, providing his critical assistance. Then the rebels would be strong enough to march on Port-au-Prince.

It is sad, really, to read Bazelais' urgent letters to this insignificant person who, so to speak, never existed—even though the Iron Coast call to arms of the previous August had been attributed to him. Cléovil Modé was a myth whose name

President Salomon had used against Bazelais. It is true that myths belong to everyone, especially in revolution.

Meanwhile, Miragoâne, where that morning it had looked like a town festival was taking place, took on entirely different atmosphere that afternoon. Word was circulating that a bloody battle that had taken place at Pont, just two hours away. Several Miragoânais had accompanied Boileau Laforest on a mission to get rid of a tyrant Commander of an adjacent district who was camped near Pont with a hundred men, and so the town was ambient with anxiety. Before long, a dispatch came announcing that the enemy had been chased out of Pont, and that among the "soldiers of the revolution" there was only one wounded, Hannibal Beaugé, of Port-au-Prince. He was one of the finest shooters among the exiles—who were all excellent shooters.

But long before the official dispatch, Boileau took the trouble of announcing his victory to the people by rushing in on his horse at a full gallop and shouting at every corner:

"We beat 'em!"

A fortified post was immediately established at Pont under the command of Gélus Bienaimé.

The next day, the 28 March, troops arrived and tried unsuccessfully to retake Pont. Gélus Bienaimé was wounded and gave command over to the famous Désormes Gresseau. The government troops—the "invaders", as they were called—attacked again on the 29. On the 30, the sloops *Equality* and *Raynaud* docked in the port and soldiers started to disembark at Salt Spring. On the morning of Saturday, 31 March, the barricade in the Detour was suddenly attacked by the presidential guard, who didn't fall back until after three hours of heated battle.

It should be said that President Salomon didn't lose a minute in this critical time; he took the offensive with vigour and a determined promptness that disconcerted the exiles. Still, Bazelais reassured them that, according to his correspondents in Port-au-Prince, the disgusted President was looking for his opportunity to abandon power and leave the country…

In the meanwhile, the siege of the city was undertaken by the attacking army, which had grown to at least 7,000 men. Within a fortnight, Désormes Gresseau, though victorious, had to abandon Pont, which was too far away, and established a post at Creek's Crossroads, which is only a kilometre from Miragoâne. Again their communications with the headquarters were vulnerable to being cut off and the Chief of Operations ordered that they return to town. In the interval they lost two of their number: Etienne Supplice and Charles Lassège, both riddled with bullets. Miragoâne mourned the loss of Turenne Sorel and Cléobule Lamarre.

The besieging troops—acting under the orders of Secretary of State François Manigat, delegate of the government, and of Generals Anselme Prophète, Henry Piquant, Vériquain, Paul-Emile Laporte, Pétion Pierre André and Plaisil Rock, the District Commander of Nippes who had fled from the house of Ahrendts in a small boat—the government's troops occupied the Detour in the west side of town, the New City and surrounding area in the south, and Saint-Romme in the east; on the north side, sloops were pummelling the town with cannonballs as cannons stationed on islets pounded the north-west. In addition, the troops had cut off water flow to the town's two fountains. The people had to resort to using well water. Deprivation took hold, and disease came with it.

Even the simplest minds could see that revolutions are an unpleasant business.

Indeed, never before had such a heroic, emotional and bloody drama unravelled in front of such a naïve audience. These few men of chimerical spirit, confined to the middle of a town, were pressed, squeezed, bombarded and sprayed point-blank with bullets by an overwhelming army—but still resisted. For ten months, they resisted not only cannonballs, bullets and fire, but also disease, fatigue, hunger and despair; they soldiered on to the last possible day, too proud to simply surrender as they were asked—even if some considered it. Each man knew that in a flash his glory might come in a grandiose death, a death that would one day testify in favour of his race, which had in the past been despised precisely because of its excessive love of life, its smug subservience to its instincts and its sickly inability to tell the truth…

The losses of the exiles numbered ninety. Ninety-one had arrived originally, but one of them, Demosthenes Fils-Aimé had deserted at Port Morant under the flimsy pretext of wanting to find a cup of coffee before getting on board…

To the stated number, there must be added two or three Cubans, who were never quite sure what they were looking for in Miragoâne. These unfortunates represented the comedic element in the romantic drama in which they found themselves, but the type of heartbreaking comedy that only real life knows how to produce. Over the course of nearly ten months, the siege of Miragoâne—which has become as famous as that of Troy—the poor Cubans were sent from one post to another, never able to make themselves heard nor hear one another. Finally, they ended up at the post of Kenscoff Sr., who spoke Spanish. Kenscoff, the old grouch, flatly refused to talk to them.

At one point, the Cubans were with Romulus, who was temporarily in charge of Fort Reflection. The only reason Romulus was able to command such a critical post was that his rank of general was maintained by the Chief of Operations. Our friend was thus taken in as an exile, all of whom were generals, in principle. As for many of the young men and fathers of families that fought admirably at Miragoâne—they were her citizens.

In the meantime, bullets and grapeshot rained down on the town; battles were followed by battles and fires by fires. The outposts of the besieging army, protected by solid ramparts erected in the night-time, were five minutes from the post of Epaminondas Desroches at the Detour, which they bombarded at all hours. The rebels' headquarters had been moved to the southern limit of Main Street and was now under the command of Désormes Gresseau. It was at an equal distance from the attackers, who were well-established at Fort Brice. At some point the two camps met to deliberate.

Much earlier, the women, children, elderly and insane had begun to leave the town. As far back as April, a first batch had left on an American brig, which had been in the harbour since its loading was disrupted by the events of 27 March.

From the consulate, in the embrasure of a window, Mr. Trévier had watched this first exodus. He watched his wife, his mother and his young Paul board a ship. Then, just as the vessel set off, his heart beat to bursting and his eyes filled with tears when he saw a young woman standing at the bow blowing him kisses and a little hand waving desperately to him.

When the brig had gone two kilometres from the port it was headed off by the *Equality*—a few days later it was courteously towed to Port-au-Prince.

Mr. Trévier was still at the consulate's window when explosions went off at the Detour, at Bel-Air, at the New City and at the Spanish fountain. This told him that the town was still being attacked from all sides.

The *Raynaud* infiltrated the harbour and started firing on the post on the Islet, composed of ten exiles under the command of Duperrier Cazeau. This post had already withstood a battle against those in the barricades of the Detour, who had thrown bombs and bullets over the strip of sea that separated them until Epaminondas Desroches, though overworked at his post at the entrance of the Detour at the foot of the mountain, and surrounded by more than a thousand regular troops, succeeded with eight others in breaking free, causing several of their oppressors to bite the dust, and many others to flee. At the same time a fire broke out in a house on the Islet. Duperrier Cazeau thus thought he was finished, and faced it all with a resolution of sheer courage, with the most admirable sangfroid. He forced the *Raynaud* to retreat, silenced the unit at Morne Blanc, brought in the combatants from the Detour, and turned their guns onto the barricade, all the while partly enveloped in flames with burning houses collapsing around him.

That day, Duperrier Cazeau and Epaminondas Desroches stepped into the ranks of the most celebrated warriors of the ages...

From the southwest-facing balcony of the consulate, around seven o'clock in the evening, Mr. Trévier witnessed the destruction of his shop on the Islet, where his thirty-five hundred pounds of coffee and batch of cocoa were all burned up in the night—a loss worth over fifteen thousand dollars.

The unlucky merchant didn't complain, didn't groan, didn't denounce. A few days later, he just asked the American consular officer to ask the Central Committee for permission to be sent with the next batch of women and children refugees to the French consulate in hopes that the French consular officer would negotiate their release.

The Central Committee refused to authorize the request, and even seized the opportunity to invite Mr. Trévier "to come take part in the defence of the city and its threatened interests, in the example of Mr. Turgeau Roc, Mr. Louis Bardinal and Mr. Seymour Gros, all of whom had recently been released from the French consulate."

Mr. Trévier shrugged his shoulders, but he felt violated when he learned that his shop had been pillaged by the American reserves stationed on the Seaside Road. The Central Committee had condoned this act with the decorative metaphor: *requisitions*.

After the American consular officer had fled the town along with the French consular officer, the parish priest and the women and children refugees on board the *Sentinel* under the French flag, Mr. Trévier, having noticed that the American consulate had become a target for the unit at Morne-Blanc and the cannons of the *Equality*, came up with a clever plan: one fine morning he took his suitcase, crossed the plaza, and moved back into his rickety home, which had been kept up by his faithful old maid, Altina, who had looked after Mr. Trévier since his wife had left.

Although it was known at the revolutionary headquarters that Mr. Trévier had gone back to his home, it was nothing to worry about. To the Commandant, who said he wanted to take rigourous measures to force this headstrong citizen to take his place among the ramparts, Bazelais responded with these four words:

"Leave that man alone."

Mr. Trévier did more. After learning that Boileau, himself having just barely recovered from a serious wound, had just lost his mother, Mr. Trévier went, quite openly, to visit him.

That afternoon, Mr. Trévier learned how his "requisitioned" logwood had been used—to build barricades for the besiegers, as much as for the besieged. The majority, however, had been burned, plain and simple.

The sad merchant couldn't help but sigh:

"So this is what I've worked for…It was to witness this that I sacrificed year after year… My God, how costly it is to be Haitian! …All my efforts are annihilated forever. It's difficult, really too difficult…"

This development was so painful for Mr. Trévier that he was suddenly lightheaded and overwhelmingly weary. Returning home, the poor merchant threw himself on the makeshift bed of sheets that Altina had laid out for him in the dining room—the upstairs bedroom had been destroyed by the projectiles that passed by at every instant.

When Altina brought her master the usual small plate of cod the merchant was shivering on his bed and didn't touch the meal. Mr. Trévier had a fever—a burning fever.

VIII

A WEEK PASSED, and then another, and another again.

The sufferings of the siege began to increase. Food rations were running low.

One day, Romulus was on his way to the headquarters when he ran into Octavius Merlin, who was passing through on his way to the perilous post at La Croix. Merlin told him that Etienne Trévier, after returning home, had fallen sick and, without the careful attention of Dr. Etienne, would surely have died.

"Well! I'll go see him," said Romulus, whose robust health could withstand anything.

To avoid the bullets of Anselme Prophète's sharpshooters, who were hidden behind the mountain thickets that descended all the way to Nippes Road, Romulus went to the headquarters by way of a path through the bushes surrounding the Croix des Martyrs.

As soon as he was announced, Bazelais welcomed him. The Chief of Operations' once pale face had turned a sickly yellow, and his eyes, formerly bright and full of hopes, were now dull.

Though the revolutionary leader had heard that the town of Jérémie had taken up arms, and that Jacmel had followed, his physical depression was such that his mental faculties seemed to be shrouded in a stagnant vapour—but his soul proved unconquerable.

He said to Romulus, in a monotone voice, handing him a letter:

"Your presence is needed at the Spanish Fountain where you'll be of great assistance to General Bigaille. Saran, your fellow citizen, will replace you at Fort Reflection."

Romulus gave the military salute and left. He passed along the dishevelled galleries of Main Street—staying out of the view of the occupants of Fort Brice, who would surely shoot at him. Bypassing the marketplace, he went straight to Mr. Trévier's house.

The merchant no longer had a fever, but his legs and feet were so swollen that he couldn't take two steps.

"The cured meats and well water are killing me," he said when he saw Romulus come in.

"What do you want?" said Romulus, who then repeated a phrase that he often heard the exiles say: "War is war!" Then he added: "Octavius sends a thousand greetings."

"Thank you."

Mr. Trévier, having noticed the way Romulus was eyeing a plate of rice and cod, which sat on the table, said to him:

"Attack at will, General."

The General didn't wait for this order to be given twice.

The plate had been prepared, superbly, and with a bit of bacon, by Altina.

"My, my! You have good things here…that's the truth," Romulus cried, his mouth full.

"Yes," said Mr. Trévier, "my wife, before leaving, had the foresight to store provisions under the stairs, which were admirably guarded by Altina against those looters."

"Nothing better than a good wife."

"That's why you have two," said Mr. Trévier.

"Certainly," Romulus replied. "Father Le Marguer, at one time, tried to get me to abandon one for the other. I refused outright. The Church herself teaches that we shouldn't continually indulge on fats—that on Fridays, Ember days and vigils, we must subsist on lean."

"And so it is," Mr. Trévier interrupted, laughing whole-heartedly at Romulus' delusion, "you indulge on fats with Virginia and subsist on lean with Isménie."

"That's it!" Romulus agreed. He winked and added: "You understand, Etienne, that if a stew is something good, a bit of herring is not bad either. Unfortunately, since all this started, I've had to fast."

"Where are they then, your wives?" Mr. Trévier asked.

"In Port-au-Prince! They left before 27 March because of Toussaint and Boyer's arrests. My younger children left at the same time as Mrs. Trévier back in April."

"Then you are all alone, like me."

"Not entirely. My son Christophe, who was the cargo manager on your schooner, is here. He's with Rénélique in the New City, and he's good with a rifle. But I've lost Rothschild, poor devil; he died at La Croix, with a bullet through the heart."

He said this matter-of-factly, as if describing an everyday occurrence, adding:

"My three houses burned down along with everything in them."

"Poor Romulus!"

"Don't say 'poor Romulus'; as long as the principles of the Revolution succeed, that's what matters."

"And what are the 'principles of the Revolution'?" Mr. Trévier asked maliciously.

The former commissioner thought for a moment, grimaced, and finally said nothing.

He didn't know.

After a moment, he mentioned that he'd like to drink something that wasn't well water.

Mr. Trévier yelled:

"Altina, rum!"

Romulus' face took on an ecstatic expression.

Altina came in a placed a carafe of firewater on the table. The former commissioner poured himself what we'd refer to as "three-fingers" of rum, which he savoured slowly, his eyes lost in the beyond.

When he came back to reality he cried energetically:

"Etienne, you are a man that I love...I would give my very life for you."

Mr. Trévier smiled and asked him:

"Who's commanding the post on the Islet?"

"Duperrier Cazeau the Younger. Unfortunately he got such a bad wound that we don't think he'll make it. All the same, Dr.

Etienne is hoping to save him. Today, Talleyrand Laroche is in charge of the post."

"There are famous men around," Mr. Trévier said with admiration.

Romulus jumped in:

"And at the Detour, today? And at La Croix? And Fort Reflection? And Fort Némorin? Everywhere, they are all famous men! And in the New City? Rénélique, man, hey! Who don't know 'im? And Désormes Gresseau, bro, who cuh' beat 'im? Every time the enemy breaks into the New City or tries to attack around the mountain down into Nippes Road, it's Désormes who comes out and scatters them to pieces, sends them back to their trenches. The invaders are forced to recognize that Miragoâne is impregnable."

"That is to say, that she is valiantly and admirably defended," Mr. Trévier reflected. "The town is so pregnable that the government's forces have broken in many times. I saw a column get as far as Bel-Air, where they cut off communication between Némorin and the post in the church, who found themselves overtaken from behind. And yet, Mr. Paulémon Berthaud, with three or four men, appeared and took less than ten minutes to break up and chase away the column of over three hundred men. I'm not without sympathy for the exiles, but I admire the effort of the government's troops."

"But at Reflection, at four in the morning the other day, the enemy made it into our ramparts; and the four of us, Joseph Lamour, Saran, the Cuban Manuel and myself, we forced them back. The exiles of the post were all sick."

"That's nice, Romulus."

"What do you want?" Romulus said proudly. "We're fighting for ideas, we are!"

"You're still at Fort Reflection?"

"No. This afternoon I was transferred to the Spanish Fountain, under the command of Succés Bigaille. This morning we sent troops to Saint-Romme, so the enemy is probably concentrating their efforts there."

And he added, looking at the carafe of rum:

"I'll come to see you often, Etienne."

"Who is in charge at Fort Reflection?" Mr. Trévier asked.

"Pio Rigaud. But, since he's sick, I've been given command."

"Are there any other Miragoânais at Fort Reflection?"

"Only one, Saran, who replaced me. He was made Division General, since he showed valour in the various assaults we've made since March."

"I don't believe it!" said Mr. Trévier. "Who would have ever imagined that there was the stuff of heroes in Saran? Such a polite boy."

"Ah! Events make the man," said Romulus, rapping the floor with the butt of his rifle.

"And Octavius, he's doing well?"

"Very well. He's stationed at La Croix with Loctamar Mayard and Mathurin Legros. He's the one that told me you were ill."

"Yes, I was in a terrible state when he came to see me last week."

At that moment, five in the afternoon, the bombardment seemed to intensify on the side of the ramparts and a lot of shooting was taking place toward the southeast.

"Things are heating up around Reflection and La Croix," Romulus said, getting to his feet. "M'off... I have to report to my post, especially since I think the Spanish Fountain is short on men. I expected this attack; all this morning I heard bursts that weren't directed at us going off at regular intervals—around noon we learned it was Manigat decimating the besieging army, and we figured they'd soon increase their attack. Good bye."

Guns were now firing constantly from the line at Bel-Air...

"Ah!" said Romulus, already in the street. "Paul Berthaud has been attacked. See you tomorrow, Etienne. God willing!"

"Until tomorrow."

And Romulus carefully made his way to his post at the Spanish Fountain, which was behind the prison, and which was towered over by the church. On the church's portico a rampart under the command of Alexandre David was set up to protect the northern part of the town.

The combat lasted two hours before the besiegers were pushed back by a heavy rainfall.

Around seven o'clock, after the downpour, someone knocked desperately on Mr. Trévier's door.

"Who's there?"

A weak voice replied:

"It's me, Octavius, I'm wounded."

Altina went to open the door and then returned followed by Merlin who was supported by an exile.

Poor Octavius had been hit in the shoulder with a piece of shrapnel. He was placed in a cot and Altina dressed his wound as well as their resources would allow. The wound wasn't fatal; Merlin soon inquired about the tempting rice and cod dish that had been forgotten on the table.

The exile said that he had the same idea as Merlin; Altina served them both a good dinner, after which they reverently downed a cup of rum each.

The exile was a man with a melancholic disposition, one of those beings marked with the fatality that comes with suffering injustice. After he was done drinking, he went to the door that led into the courtyard of the house; there, he observed the weather for a moment. The night was thick and there wasn't a star in the black sky. A wispy rain was falling.

From time to time, some gunshots sounded from the ramparts of the insurgents, meant to keep the besiegers at bay. They were the only sound that interrupted the unsettling silence that hovered over the town, the poor little town lost to obscurity and crushed by a steel grip.

The exile went back into the dining room and sat down near the table in the faint glow of the candle that lit the room. After a moment in silence, he told those present that he was a poor man, a husband and a father of two children whom he cherished with all his heart; that he was forced into the life of an exile because his brother, who was suspected of Bazelaisism, had been shot by Jean-Jumeau in Gonaïves along with the fourteen victims of 6 May 1882; that he personally was never interested in politics; that as a store clerk he eked out a living for his small family, which had to struggle through poverty at this time, since his wife was sweet and kind but didn't have much initiative; and that it was in the fear of prison and execution that he had taken refuge in a consulate and then left for Jamaica without a cent. After spending a year in hardship and poverty he accepted the proposition of the Liberal Party, who offered to take him back to his country, explaining that everything had been prepared for their reception.

"In effect," he added bitterly, "Mr. Bazelais couldn't have said it better; we were received admirably."

The exile lamented that the rebels' near-evacuation of the plaza in the first half of April hadn't taken place; and he regretted not having fled at that time with Diogenes Bras, Magnan and Joachim Nicolas in their little rowboat.

Merlin seethed.

"When you're engaged in a revolutionary undertaking, like this one," he yelled, "the fate of each person is bound to the fate of all his companions; by saving themselves, like they did, these gentlemen acted in a way that I won't even qualify for the time being—but I don't respect them!"

"They didn't save themselves," the exile replied in a gloomy tone; "it was with the Chief of Operations' consent that they took their aquatic retreat, because they were against the idea of the interior evacuation planned for 10 April. You'll remember what happened at Creek's Crossroads, we should have returned to the town then, as virtually everyone wanted to. In any case," the exile sighed, "Magnan, Bras and Joachim are in Kingston now."

"Really!" Mr. Trévier exclaimed. "They were able to cross the channel on that frail little rig?"

"Yes. An enemy officer told us so during the last ceasefire."

And the unfortunate exile cursed Bazelais and Boileau Laforest, who had lured him into this trap in Miragoâne where he now anguished—forgetting, the poor man, how many in Kingston he personally had convinced to come along, saying with the rest that it was preferable to die from a bullet in Haiti than to waste away from starvation in exile.

In the face of this distress, Mr. Trévier turned his head and thought about how he too had lost everything and how his poor wife and his little Paulémon were on the streets in Port-au-Prince with no one to support them.

"Except," he said to himself, "my poor dear Eugenia has smarts, she does."

And Mr. Trévier set to thinking about how he could get to Anselme Prophète's camp in the night-time. Unfortunately, his swollen legs and feet had him stuck in one place for the present.

"A bit more rum to warm you up?" Mr. Trévier proposed amicably.

"With pleasure."

The exile drank, saluted, and reluctantly left to return to his post, his rifle on his right shoulder.

Maybe five minutes after he had left, Mr. Trévier said to Merlin:

"And in such a state of mind, he goes back without a second thought. What keeps him here?"

"Honour," Merlin replied.

"President Salomon would welcome him with open arms," said Mr. Trévier.

"It's true," said Merlin, "if he went to him he would gain his life, a title and also… disgrace!"

"And then after that," said Mr. Trévier, "there will still be people to challenge the high Haitian ideals."

"Because there is no justice," Merlin murmured and fell into a deep sleep.

The next morning, Mr. Trévier wrote a note concerning Merlin to Dr. Etienne, who was still living in his house with two or three friends. He was one of Miragoâne's most respected citizens, and had a heart of gold. Dr. Etienne had a special interest in Merlin because, since he had been the Chief of Financial Administration until 27 March and Merlin had been a manager, the young man had worked under the doctor's orders; and so, despite the bombardment which continued unabated, the doctor made his way to Mr. Trévier's house, equipped with all the medicine he thought he might need. He carefully dressed his young friend's wound and gave Altina a few small packets of powder, explaining how to get Mr. Trévier back on his feet. After chatting for a minute, the old doctor left, telling them that he planned to get out of the country as soon as possible.

In fact, the next night, Dr. Etienne and his friends left the town by the Saint-Romme path.

Two or three other Miragoânais who didn't want to fight, and who had been part of a company of volunteers, made it to the enemy camp where, like other "deserters", they were treated with respect.

On the other hand, an act of self-sacrifice and devotion should also be noted—two young men, Joseph Lamour of

Jacmel and Hugon of Jérémie, had broken into the starving town where they had given their enthusiastic support to those men that they admired...

IX

AND THE SIEGE CONTINUED. Days turned to nights and back to days without a break in the gunfire, without the fighting diminishing, and without the besieged losing an inch of terrain.

People on both sides wanted an end to this painful and bloody battle. After every major attack new cemeteries were struck around Miragoâne...

Since the start of the hostilities, on two occasions the French diplomat from Port-au-Prince had intervened with a bid for peace. The first time the French legation chancellor, Mr. Boulanger, was sent to Miragoâne; the second time the diplomat went there himself. President Salomon, putting aside all his pride and thinking, as the true Chief of State, of nothing but hurrying along the conclusion of the rebellion, consented to paying off the war debts and protecting all of the insurgents against abuse until they could safely leave the country—he even offered them a steamer for their escape.

Mathurin Legros, in his dispatch to the commanders of the various posts on 14 December, alleged, in good faith no doubt, that Mr. Burdel had left on 8 May with a message to Salomon accepting this proposal. The truth was that Bazelais, not knowing whether the other towns had taken up arms, and imagining that the government was being kept at bay, avoided responding altogether. He didn't refuse but he didn't accept either—he tried to buy some time by demanding modifications to the government's diplomatic corps.

Mr. Burdel promised to return in a fortnight and report on the President's intentions. In the meantime, the town of Jérémie had taken up arms on 23 May. This convinced Salomon to accept the complicated modifications proposed by Bazelais. The French diplomat presented the proposal to the Spanish ambassador, Mr. Garrido, to sign. He refused because there was no mention of the insurrection taking place in Jérémie.

Mr. Garrido realized the government was trying to trick the exiles, using a wholly dishonest tactic. President Salomon told him that if Bazelais knew about the uprising in Jérémie he would take the opportunity to make additional demands or refuse the settlement altogether. It was critical that things didn't turn out that way.

The noble Spaniard stood firm, the French diplomat insisted, and finally President Salomon renounced his offer. And that's why Mr. Burdel never returned to Miragoâne…

Months passed and every day lives were snuffed out in the besieged town. Disease took Brutus Casimir, Turenne Guerrier, Joseph Muller, Pio Rigaud and his son Turenne, the always valiant Désormes Gresseau, Devimeux Lys, whose fighting skills had won him the admiration of his companions; and finally, Moulite Tuffet, Blain, Rincher and Perpignand followed the others to the tomb. Balls and bullet had taken many: Lucéna

Léveillé, the adolescent Dantès Martin, Planchet Audigé, Prévost Chavanne, Charles Geffrard and Gélus Bienaimé all fell under the enemies' cannonballs; one shot had killed Labossière and Antoine Nicholas at the Spanish Fountain; Paulémon Berthaud, Chanlatte and Roy were killed, and the Miragoânais Saran who, like Romulus, was incapable of understanding the ideas for which he was fighting, had recently been killed by a bullet.

Almost all of the wounded had now succumbed to their injuries. There were no doctors and especially no medicine. Wounds that could easily have been treated turned gangrenous for want of antiseptic. Hannibal Beaugé, after recovering from a ball to the chest, was again debilitated from a wounded leg. The Miragoânais Antoine Lully operated on him with a cured-meat merchant's knife, and in the end had to cut it off at the tibia with a handsaw. Nonetheless, after bravely facing this terrible operation, Hannibal Beaugé breathed his last...

As for the besiegers, on 22 September, after a well-executed attack, their bodies littered the streets. Henry Piquant, who was admired for his courage and daring, on the *Sentinel* followed by the two other government vessels, made it all the way into the little harbour and attempted a landing; but Constantine Rigaud, commander of Fort-Malet, though wounded in the hip and suffering from illness, prevented the raid. Rigaud orchestrated this memorable defence from a rocking chair, aided by Auguste Kavanagh and a decrepit old cannon, as well as six other companions who advanced into the sea up to their belts, shooting rifles all the while. Among the six was the Jérémian

Hugon who died in the incident. After the epic battle, where Henry Piquant was mortally wounded, the boats had to retreat and the *Sentinel*, the hull of which had been damaged with bullets, was left to sink among the mangroves of Salt Spring...

After this considerable effort the besiegers began to get discouraged, but the exiles held hope—they held hope until the end.

It was at this point that a local medium came to offer his services to the besiegers, to put an end to this terrible war that seemed like it would go on forever.

An *houngan* (voodoo priest) named Ti-Blanc approached Anselme Prophète, and offered to help him. He planned to enter Miragoâne by himself and to assassinate Boyer Bazelais —with Bazelais gone the war would be over.

"But how do you intend to infiltrate the town?" Anselme Prophète asked, intrigued.

"That's my secret," Ti-Blanc said smoothly.

He was promised a large sum, and Ti-Blanc set about on his little project the following night. Around midnight he left Fort Brice on foot. In his hand he had one of those large wooden triangles that are put around the necks of domestic animals to prevent them from getting through fences and into private yards. After a few steps he put the *tribart* around his neck and headed in the direction of the revolutionary headquarters, grunting energetically. The *houngan* told himself that the exiles would take him for a pig and ignore him, and that it would thus be easy to get close to Bazelais and stab him. That was where Ti-Blanc was mistaken. At that moment a pig was more valuable to the insurgents than a man; when the sentinel of the barricade protecting the headquarters—under the command of Brave Béliard since the death of Désormes Gresseau—heard the far-off grunting of an approaching pig, he hurried to wake his companions, telling them the excellent blessing that was coming their way, an unexpected relief from heaven. The best shooters among the exiles silently armed their rifles, all the while imagining sausages, pork chops, and delicious bacon. The three best shooters among the exiles spotted, not ten steps away from the barricade, a quadruped trying to find an entrance to the neighbouring house of the Chief of Operations. They fired and the animal collapsed—with a human cry. The entire post rushed toward the beast and found themselves looking on the cadaver of Ti-Blanc, drenched in his own blood, the *tribart* still around his neck.

How disappointing!

The poor exiles thought they had killed a pig, alas! They had only killed one more man.

In the first few days of October, Mr. Trévier, feeling fairly comfortable on his feet, decided to leave town. He was waiting for nightfall to put his plan into action. That afternoon his friends Merlin and Romulus came to visit him. He welcomed them with his usual cordiality.

Romulus began by asking for some rum, which was hastily served to him, and which he gulped down delightedly. Then, under its soothing influence, he began to talk about his dreams for the future, when Bazelais would be president and he, Romulus, would be District Commander of Nippes…

Merlin, for his part, embraced dreams similarly full of charm: he saw himself becoming Minister of Education and thought about the speaking tours he would go on and the praise he would receive from the prestigious Chief of State, who he had the pleasure of serving.

Oh! This bright future he longed for with all his being!

Meanwhile, Mr. Trévier, full of joy at the thought of soon seeing his loved ones, set about preparing a modest meal for his friends, after which he offered them some champagne.

Romulus thought he was joking. Champagne in Miragoâne in October 1883? That could hardly be possible.

"You know, Etienne," he said solemnly, "I'm a serious man."

"It's because I know it, O Romulus, that I'm offering you champagne—a bit of Veuve Clicquot that Octavius knows well, since he often made acquaintance with it while he was here recovering, taking his time."

"You mean there's some left!" Merlin shouted.

"Three bottles!"

"So Altina was pulling my leg when she swore to Saint La Mercie that I had finished it off."

"You have to understand that Altina is a superior housekeeper—she divided up the remainder and she didn't lie when she swore to Saint La Mercie that you finished it off— you had indeed finished off the portion determined for you."

"Ah! Octavius!" Romulus said accusingly. "You never told me about that."

"I apologize, Romulus," said Merlin, "but I was so content! And you know that when you're happy you can easily forget your friends."

"That's comforting," Mr. Trévier said as he carefully uncorked the round-bodied bottle.

And once their glasses were filled, Mr. Trévier clinked his with those of his friends, saying:

"To your health, sirs, and to the fulfilment of your wishes!"

But Octavius Merlin, as if in a sudden crisis, raised his glass and said frantically:

"I drink to the Haitian man without fear and without reproach, who, for seven months, has guided immemorial defence of Miragoâne with a talent and genius beyond the scope of praise. I drink to Boyer Bazelais."

Romulus, not to be outdone, collected his thoughts for a moment and then cried:

"I drink to the conservation of the most illustrious man among us, who presides over the destiny of our town. I drink to General Boyer Bazelais, protector of principles, enemy of tyranny and father to us all!"

After that, they went down the hall into a room in the house that was always cool in that hour of the afternoon. The three Miragoânais sat together and had another glass of champagne without worrying about the bombardment that was taking place, as it had become a part of their daily lives.

They calmly recounted old Miragoânais stories, always the same, the fancies of old men from long ago, like Racine Derenoncour, Mérard Hogu and Emile Manuel, who believed that the town belonged to them; then they moved onto more recent times. Merlin recounted, for the thousandth time, the jokes and antics of the Lépine brothers: Chateaubriand, Nemours and Lord Byron.

Finally, certain specifics of the siege came up; they spoke of Adamar Passé, fishing philosophically on the frontline, under the fire of the sloops and forts; of Talleyrand Laroche, and how he loved horsemeat, and would go from fort to fort collecting contributions; of the passion to hang onto one's rights, and on that theme they spoke of Kenscoff, never wounded though he'd seen as much combat as anyone, and was always a visible target with his bright red shirt and wide-brimmed hat. They spoke of Dantès Mathon, who had turned the head of the beautiful Mrs. T... Finally, the conversation turned to the exile Robert Jean-Pierre who had defected to the enemy...

Suddenly, Romulus and Merlin leapt to their feet and let out a terrible cry. Altina ran in.

Mr. Trévier had been hit in the head with a musket ball and thrown to the floor, his brains scattered about.

His still-warm body was stretched out on the floorboards. His head was almost entirely crushed. Only his lower jaw was left intact. Altina, on her knees beside this victim of the errors of others, cried desperately and in vain—cried out to Mrs. Trévier in Port-au-Prince, and asked "why did they do this to him?"

Romulus and Merlin stayed late into the evening and watched over what was left of Mr. Trévier. They were deeply moved by the qualities of the man that Miragoâne had just lost. They knew his high moral and intellectual value, his patience, his kindness, his love of work, his unwavering strength of character…

And with every memory of the deceased, Romulus and Merlin cried—they cried the most noble, the most pure tears they had ever produced in their lives.

The next morning, the two Miragoânais, despite the impossibility of the timing, succeeded in locating a carpenter enrolled in the volunteer corps, who agreed to build a coffin, because it was for *Missta* Etienne, who had always been good to him.

Romulus and Merlin paid their last respects to their friend who they had, with great difficulty, brought to the cemetery themselves.

There, they placed the coffin in the crypt where Almonacy Trévier was already interred. Then they returned to their respective posts.

X

Unrelenting, the battle went on. Bazelais, aged, gaunt, eroded by disease and sorrows, still maintained his faculties, and everyone agreed that he still gave his orders with the same precision, the same foresight that brought him so much honour. He had just gone to bed for the last time. Some days earlier, on the subject of the new defensive measures in response to the barricades that the besiegers had put up in the neighbourhood of the revolutionary headquarters, he had written to Loctamar Mayard, head of the La Croix post: "I now know, in the air I seem to sense the precursor to an upcoming resolution."

In his mind, the resolution would come about by the Jacmelians who were now in arms, and would come and liberate Miragoâne. He was mistaken; the resolution he sensed in the air was impending death, the mysterious death, imposing and sweet, that was advancing slowly and would bring him peace: the true, sacred peace of the tomb.

Right up to the last moment, as not to discourage his companions, he was able to compose himself serenely—though his soul was hardened.

An hour before he closed his eyes forever, Talleyrand Laroche, who had just been with him, announced to the bed-ridden Mathurin Legros that the General was doing better.

Such was the cup of bitterness he drank straight to the dregs! As a martyr, he suffered to command, without real power, a band of equals, of brothers! He alone knew that he been forced to show this patience, this mildness, this angelic leniency in the face of overwhelming criticism, because he had failed to deliver a swift victory. Generous souls are rare in this world, and those that stood up for their cause were not all elites like the Laroches, the Elies, the Béliards, Duperrier Cazeau, Epaminondas Desroches, Kenscoff the Elder, Ulysses Fourreau, Jules Arbuthnott, Constantine Rigaud, Loctamar Mayard, Dantès Mathon, Franck Solages, Arécius Rénélique and a few others.

One Dardinac threw his demotion from District Commander back in Bazelais' face with the coarseness of a sugar cane farmer, ending his letter with: "General Boyer Bazelais, I need not to hide the fact that I infinitely regret having followed the politics of a man whom I never knew, and who never knew me …You are a fool."

Bazelais swallowed this, and wrote back at length to Dardinac, trying to explain himself…

A former colleague in the House—quite a character! — Berthaud the Younger, harshly accused Bazelais of having deceived him; and to punish himself for having "believed in such a man" Berthaud blew his brains out.

Charles Desroches wrote in his journal about this death, and that of Lassègue, killed by a bullet at the outset: "There go two brilliant minds, victims of an unfortunate expedition, poorly carried out by a vain and incapable man."

That's how they spoke about him behind his back.

And he knew it. And he took it quietly, stoically, always holding hope.

Ah! He would have been well acquainted with the agony of suspense.

If anyone ever had the right to build on the promises of men, it was Boyer Bazelais. Followers from across the Republic had come to him like the smoke of incense to an idol! He was the providential man, divinely created by special decree to save Haiti. He thus had metaphysical reasons to believe that the whole nation would rise in his support when they heard that he was on war footing in Miragoâne!

But still, he didn't expect it. Countries that don't consider their citizens can't rely on a person; true citizens don't wait for a deliverer, they do what must be done themselves! This type of liberalism was a trap. It went by the name of liberalism but was just another type of absolutism, yet another source of social hierarchy...

If now, at his ultimate hour, he could see them, these bourgeois that had worshipped him, all the while humouring Salomon, bending their spines before their all-powerful Master; if he could read their servile messages, covered in their signatures, deposited at the feet of the Father of the Fatherland; if he could hear the repulsive terms they had given to foreign commerce, in order to fight the president's battle; if he could contemplate the political bodies that wretchedly declared their devotion to this contemptible Tiberius Caesar...

Maybe, then, he had realized that while some people placed their dignity in the love of liberty, others put all their energy into servitude. And considering the just words of President Salomon that "the Liberal Party, in the heat of their resentment, drew their power from an imaginary source," Bazelais would have understood the absurdity of his efforts. In sum, he had worked tirelessly, sacrificing his own life and those of many remarkable men only to overturn his own movement, plaguing the Republic with mourning and enriching the economy of Martinique, its convicts and exotic marshlands.

But he couldn't have seen, he couldn't have known—he couldn't have imagined this!

In his abstract, revolutionary, idealist mind he told himself that men were good and their nature was moral. With his head drooping under the weight of responsibility and his heart battered by the agony of suspense, he gave up his spirit on that morning of 27 October 1883, at the age of fifty, while the sun rose to embrace the desolate town with its magnificent rays, while the fracas of canons, bullets and grapeshot continued...

XI

THE CENTRAL COMMITTEE and the heads of the various posts gathered that same day and unanimously elected Epaminondas Desroches as the leader of the revolutionary forces of Miragoâne.

Epaminondas Desroches was the commander of the post in the Detour, which is to say, the post that, for the past seven months, continuously held off the most determined effort of the besieging army.

How Epaminondas Desroches was able, often with only eight men, to withstand the constant bombardment of Fort Jean-Louis against the rampart comprising three cannons elevated to fifty feet in front of them, and against Fort Salomon to their side, which bombarded them day and night with a superior weapon, and finally against the numerous fortified posts set up on the mountain at the foot of which they stood, remains unexplained. What Achilles did this man contain?

Epaminondas Desroches was stocky and quarrelsome, lively and merry. In combat, especially in the first days, he would leave the ramparts and chase off the enemy by himself, right until he ran out of bullets.

Surely, it is unfortunate that the valour of such a man should be established in combat against his compatriots, but nevertheless, his true heroism must be acknowledged and ranked highly.

Apart from the Persian Wars, Greeks only ever fought against Greeks; and yet, the fame of those among them that stood out in these civil wars has survived for centuries, because patriotic writers never fail to bring outstanding accomplishments to light.

If it was only to pay homage to the most heroic of the heroes among them that Epaminondas Desroches' companions chose to make him their leader, they couldn't have made a better choice. But it seemed that, in addition to his military valour, the new leader possessed political abilities.

Once elected, he sought to put an end to the fighting which no longer had a point, Bazelais being dead.

In addition, the provision stores were all depleted. There was no more flour, no more pork, no more rice—an agent of the besieging army had managed to burn down the food warehouse.

As stated by the exile Clavius Claude, who was taken and executed at Aquin after the evacuation, it had come to the point where the besieged "were reduced to eating not only domestic animals, such as horses stolen from the enemy camp in the night-time, but also vermin, such as rats, mice, cats. They also ate birdseed, the leather that lined their trunks, and all sorts of leaves that they found in the town, using castor oil as cooking grease."

With the cooperation of the exterior revolutionary committee—whose only goal was to free Bazelais—the Jacmelian insurgents managed to commandeer the paddle-wheeler *Eider* which they christened the *Fatherland*. In the final days of October, this ship made its first appearance at Miragoâne; just as they were about to disembark, the two Jérémian commissioners unsealed a letter that they had been told not to open until that moment. It contained an order not to allow the Jérémian volunteers to disembark at Miragoâne—unless they, the Jérémian commissioners, could respond promising that not a hair on a Jérémian head would be harmed. It goes without saying that in the face of such instructions—of which no one could dispute the original character—the exiles received no aid. They couldn't even be informed of their good fortune—that they had a warship! It was the guards of the besieging army who, during their often hazardous watch, announced to the besieged that that "Black Devil" was the revolutionaries' battleship, but that it would soon be sunk by the "Dessalines", which the government had recently purchased and was in the process of heavily arming in Port-au-Prince.

So the chief of revolutionary forces at Miragoâne, thinking that the *Fatherland* would soon succeed in breaking into the harbour, prepared a letter addressed to the diplomatic corps and the consulate at Port-au-Prince, requesting their intervention "to put an end to this battle that had gone on for nearly eight months, while maintaining honourable conditions for the defenders of Miragoâne." He also decided to send a delegation of three members onboard the *Fatherland* to go and explain the situation to the comrades in Jérémie and Jacmel.

On 14 November, the *Fatherland*, with numerous Jacmelian and Jérémian volunteers on board, reappeared at Miragoâne.

The insurgents' warship, this time, immediately let two boatloads of men down into the water—the cannons and heavy artillery of the besiegers couldn't do them any harm. The *Equality* and the *Oakwood* manoeuvred to hide themselves behind the islets around Salt Spring, all the while hurling a few bullets at the *Fatherland* for good measure.

When Anselme Prophète realized that the rebels were about to receive reinforcements and rations, he was discouraged and started packing up to leave.

But Dardinac, abandoning Constantine Rigaud and Jules Arbuthnott (the other delegates who were supposed to accompany him) on shore, made it to the warship on his own under a rain of bullets.

On board, he found, among others, Magnan, Pomié and Mr. Camille Bruno. He persuaded them and the ship's captain, Bougette Pratt, to call back the rowboats, which ran the risk of being sunk at any moment, and to try for a landing that evening.

Thus, the defenders at Miragoâne watched in a stupor as the *Fatherland* headed off in the direction of Petit-Goâve.

The insurgents' ship soon encountered the *Dessalines*, which President Salomon had just commissioned to chase them down, and which treated them poorly. Instead of returning to Miragoâne that evening, the *Fatherland* went to Jérémie.

Six days later, Epaminondas Desroches took ill.

A young lawyer from Gonaïves, Mathurin Legros, who had been in command of Fort Reflection, was elected chief of revolutionary forces. As he wasn't personally an opponent of President Salomon, having been an exile under the provisional government of Herissé, some of his companions imagined that he, more than anyone, could intercede with the Chief of State.

After consulting the committee and the chiefs of each of the posts, of which six had voted against him (Loctamar Mayard, Talleyrand Laroche, Jules Arbuthnott, Brave Béliard, Titon Passé and Jean-Pierre Bazelais!), Mathurin Legros continued the negotiations that his predecessor had thought to establish. He, however, employed a new tactic to get his letter to the diplomatic corps; he addressed it to the military commission at the Detour, composed of Lajeune, Plaisit Rock, Catilina Victor, Rosa, etc.

President Salomon, having been informed that his opponents were reduced to mere phantoms and were on the verge of surrendering, responded to the diplomatic corps that the insurgents seemed to want to put themselves on the same footing as him, and that he would not condescend to accept anything less than total submission, pure and simple.

The insurgents received this response with heavy spirits. However, they refused to lay down their arms under the conditions proposed by the Chief of State—even though some among them were of the opinion that it would be worth it to put an end to the battle.

Meanwhile, disease continued to take one after another: Pinchinat Sr., Alphonse Barthole, Vincent-Guerrier Loiseau,

Modés, Charles Mathurin, Bariento, Constantine Rigaud and William Rigaud were among the dead…

Those still breathing kept up the resistance, always counting on the other towns that had taken up arms and especially on the warship of the revolution.

In the second fortnight of December, first Jérémie, then Jacmel and the Iron Coast surrendered.

The guards of the outposts of the besieging army, in their nocturnal lookouts, laughed cruelly as they announced this news to the insurgents…

In the end, a lamentable fact presented itself, annihilating the remaining hope in the souls of the defenders of Miragoâne.

In the afternoon of 7 January, the *Dessalines*, towing the *Fatherland*, dropped anchor in front of Fort Malet.

In face of this concrete image of absolute defeat the heroes understood that their time was up. Death was their best option.

"What to do, sirs?" cried Mathurin Legros.

"Evacuate the town," said Kenscoff coldly, with the support of Loctamar Mayard, Brave Béliard, Franck Solages and Déjoie —the latter of these was dying.

"But where would we go? It would be better to accept surrender. Evacuation would be the death of all of us!" Mathurin Legros exclaimed.

"We will go straight toward them," Kenscoff said resolutely. "We will go straight toward our death—since all that's left for us is to die heroically, as we've been fighting for ten months!"

"We'll evacuate then." Mathurin Legros sighed, thinking of his wife and children.

XII

AT TWO O'CLOCK the next morning, 8 January 1884, Octavius Merlin, who was manning his post at La Croix, saw a shadowy figure heading toward him from the direction of Bel-Air.

"Who goes there?" he yelled.

"It's me, General Romulus."

"Come forward."

"What is it?" the chief of the post inquired, showing himself.

"I've come to tell you that it's not necessary for you to go to Fort Némorin like you were originally told. Kenscoff is going to come by here soon and bring us all to Fort Reflection."

"What for?"

"He said we'd be in a better position to organize our exit."

"Very well."

And Romulus stayed with Merlin.

Around three o'clock, a large number of armed men, followed by women and children, all carrying luggage, arrived at La Croix.

It was a brisk morning and the sky shimmered with stars.

All told there were thirty-six exiles, and almost as many Miragoânais, including the Cubans and Joseph Lamour. Twelve sick exiles, including Luc Elie, had stayed in the town along with five or six Miragoânais in the same condition. Some women, admired for their courage and devotion, stayed at the bedsides of these unfortunates; they were Mother Massillon Roc, Mrs. Boutin and her daughter Luména, Mrs. Lamarre and her daughters Lorméla (the valiant and unshakeable) and Matoute Hogu, Miss Marie Gaubert who, during Bazelais' lifetime, had served as cook for the Chief of Operations, and Miss Tertulia Tertulien whose mother, always devoted to the exiles, had died during the siege.

"It seems," said Mayard, "that Boileau is among the sick who stayed in town."

"He was with us at Némorin," Kenscoff replied, "though he could hardly walk. With the support of a volunteer, Éléazar Milord, he headed off toward Saint-Romme, saying that he wouldn't be taken alive, and he wouldn't be taken dead either. There's no way he could have kept up."

"Alas!" Déjoie moaned, "I feel the same way. I can't take another step."

"Poor friend."

"But it seems to me, sirs," said Mayard, "that Mathurin Legros should be here with us."

"He should meet up with us at Reflection," said Romulus.

"Onward, then!"

With that word they marched on, leaving poor Déjoie behind, sitting on the ground with his back against a barricade.

At Fort Reflection, the little army met up with Mathurin Legros, who divided it up into three factions: a vanguard, which included, among others, Joseph Lamour, the two remaining Cubans, Manuel and Pedro, Romulus and Merlin; the middle guard contained most of the exiles and the rearguard was made up of a dozen Miragoânais men, protecting the women and children.

Once things were thus arranged they took to the mountain south of Fort Reflection, and after many unforeseen obstacles and various tumbles in the crevices the vanguard fell into an enemy rampart at Creek's Crossroads.

"*Carajo! Al' arma blanca!* " the two Cubans cried.

And, ultimately, they razed the rampart with their knives.

There, they found an abundance of fresh water in barrels—the poor insurgents, for whom it was like nectar, quenched their thirst until they were unable to move.

"Onward! Onward!" the yells came from all directions.

It was then that the division occurred. Some took the Pont Road, while others took the bypass of West-Savannah. The latter route was taken by Mathurin Legros, who had found a general's horse at Creek's Crossroads.

Romulus, who was worn out, looked all over for Merlin. He had lost his son Christophe—run through with a bayonet blade when they took Creek's Crossroads not a quarter of an hour earlier. Realizing that he wasn't going to find Merlin, and finding himself along on the great road of Aquinas, poor Romulus headed off toward the Duparc Coast.

The mountain was taken, for the most part, in a stampede of women and children.

The military commission in the Detour learned about the evacuation of the city from those retreating from Creek's Crossroads. Neither the commission nor the army could believe the news.

"I suspect a trap," said the ever-cautious Lajeune.

However, after much hesitation, it was decided that they would occupy the town. The "prepare for combat" was given, and the army, moving like wolves, advanced toward the rampart of Epaminondas Desroches—honourably commanded, after his departure, by Dantès Mathon.

The prestige of this rampart was such that, at the moment of their approach, generals and soldiers, overtaken by a mad panic, turned around and fled.

But the officers of the mountain posts yelled out that Desroches' rampart was unguarded. Hearing this, the generals renewed their martial attitudes and went back to the rampart, in which there wasn't even a cat—that was the case but they agreed not to speak of it.

The besieging army, encouraged by this success, set to firing shots in the air and dancing to the sound of drums, a frantic *coudiaille*.

President Salomon's Proclamation of 8 January 1884 declared: "Haitians, on the eighth of this month, government troops took the town of Miragoâne by assault…"

How brutally this impatient army descended on the extinguished Miragoâne can only be guessed. The women were mistreated; some were imprisoned, Lormé and Hogu, among others; some were whipped. The exiles, found sick or wounded

—what was going on in their souls in these terrible hours? — were dragged to their deaths. These included Talleyrand and Toussaint Laroche, Albert and Gaston Elie, Jean-Baptiste Chenet, Ulysses Fourreau, Geffrard Lucas, O'Brien, Bélomon Duvivier. Alfred Brisard, rheumatic and crippled after four months in bed, was executed in a rocking chair just as was Sam Blanchet, already swollen to agony. Déjoie was finished off at La Croix.

"Flying Columns" were sent in pursuit of the insurgents who had fled into the woods. Many of them, the suffering, the isolated, were taken.

The whole day of 8 January was nothing but an atrocious massacre: Alexandre David, Massillon Jean-Bart, Jean-Pierre Bazelais, the Miragoânais Elie Derenoncour and the last remaining Cuban were pitilessly shot along with fifteen others.

Duperrier Cazeau, the man who knew no fear, won the universal admiration of his enemies, so great was he before death.

At Port-au-Prince, that same day, at the National Palace, a dinner gala was presented to Admiral Cooper. Cooper was the commander of the American warship "Tennessee", currently in the harbour.

Mrs. Salomon had Admiral Cooper on her right and Mr. Brenor Prophète, Secretary of the Navy, on her left. On the right of His Excellency President Salomon was Mr. Langston, Minister to the United States, and on his left was Mr. Callisthenes Fouchard, Secretary of Finance.

During the course of the meal an altogether touching scene took place and moved the hearts of those present.

The *Dessalines*, decorated triumphantly, came and anchored close to Fort Islet with its prize, the *Fatherland*—the shell of which can still be seen on the north end of River Wharf.

President Salomon had reserved a special place for the captain of the Haitian cruiser, an American named Cooper who was the son of Admiral Cooper of the "Tennessee".

When Captain Cooper arrived he fell into the American Admiral's arms—as if in the final act of a play. It was too much for the president's guests. Each cried unreservedly.

Meanwhile, that day and those that followed, Haitian blood continued to flow at Miragoâne. The young people who had stayed in the town because of indifference, or naïvely trying to save their lives, alas! The young bakers, the commissioners, the water carriers, they were executed just the same as the men of the people, like Lauréus, Valdéus and Marcellus, who were all devoted to the "cause."

In the woods, the insurgents were tracked and surrounded, individually or in small groups. They fought back like lions, killing many before succumbing to their besiegers. The dead included Kenscoff Sr., Loctamar Mayard, Franck Solages, Charles Bazelais, Paul Etienne and Godefroy Noël.

Some of them, found unarmed or sick, like Succés Bigaille, Charles Desroches, Moreau, Antonin Boncy, Lascases Samson and Adamar Passé, were immediately executed. The Miragoânais combatants, led by Merlin, met the same fate.

Other exiles blew their brains out rather than being taken alive, and their bodies became food for the starving dogs that wandered the woods.

The insurgents who made it to Petit-Goâve fought a bloody battle with the town's troops, but, surrounded on all sides, they were annihilated. Some, wounded but still breathing, were also snuffed out—among others, the intrepid Rénélique, Auguste Kavanagh, Spirius Lorquet and Morel Jacob.

Only one exile was spared: Luc Elie. He did nothing for it. It was on the pressing request of President Salomon's stepdaughter that this exception was made.

Three young men of Miragoâne found mercy in the face of their conquerors: Desaix and Massillon Roc, because of their extreme youth, presumably, and Rousselin Montpérous, because of the services his father, who had been in the camp of Anselme Prophète, had rendered to the besieging army.

The last exile executed was Mathurin Legros, more than two months after the evacuation. Brought to Dufour by a brave mid-countryman named Thiocoly, who was the "manager" of a garden in the area, Mathurin Legros let himself be taken in the end, because he believed that the appeasement had been made, and in any case he had accepted the principle of submission, pure and simple.

Thiocoly managed to get out of being prosecuted for concealing an exile by pretending to be insane.

He was an old black, dressed like Deputy Cabrilho—walking barefoot, in trousers that were too big, and a big sheet for a jacket, in which he practically disappeared.

His commendable act won him the esteem of the population —and right up to his death, in 1891, Thiocoly lived as Miragoâne's spoiled child...

In the last days of the month of January, a patrol in the vicinity of Saint Michel stopped a suspicious old man.

It was Romulus.

He was taken into the city where he was interrogated. The detachment was ordered to bring him to Croix des Martyrs.

He walked bravely, his felt hat on his head.

Arriving at their destination, Romulus stood at four paces from the firing squad. On the order of the principal officer, the soldiers took aim.

The former commissioner said a short prayer, committing his spirit to God.

Then he raised his hat and yelled in a terrible voice:

"Down with the tyrant!"

"Fire!" said the commander of the firing squad.

A formidable discharge rung out and the unfortunate victim, battered with bullets and covered in blood, fell to his knees and pressed one hand to the ground.

In a raspy voice, he found the strength to exhale:

"Long live liberty!"

A soldier advanced and pressed the barrel of his carbine to Romulus' ear.

"No...no...the heart!" said Romulus, turning to the executioner with a compelling glance.

He obeyed the request and fired at the preferred spot.

This time, Romulus fell backwards, stone dead, arms crossed—facing the great blue sky.

About the Translator

Matthew Robertshaw studies history and French literature at the University of Guelph. A brief visit to the country in 2011 led him to direct his studies toward Haiti's unique history and literature. Noticing the virtual absence of English  translation, Matthew set to translating, starting with Fernand Hibbert's Romulus, and is currently working on his second translation. He lives in Cambridge, Ontario with his wife and dog.

NOTES

i Edmund Wilson, *Red, Black, Blond and Olive—Studies in Four Civilizations: Zuñi, Haiti, Soviet Russia, Israel.* (New York: Oxford, 1956), 110.

ii Napoleon Bonaparte, as quoted in Laurent Dubois, *Haiti: The Aftershocks of History*. (New York: Henry Holt, 2012), 36.

iii Michel-Rolph Trouillot, *Silencing the Past*. (Boston: Beacon, 1995), 100.

iv Dubois, *Aftershocks*, 60.

v Frederick Douglas, as quote in Dubois, *Avengers of the New World*. (Cambridge: Harvard, 2004), 305.

vi Robin Blackburn, *The Overthrow of Colonial Slavery*. (Bath: Bookcraft, 1988), 30.

vii Patrick Bellegard-Smith, *Haiti: The Breached Citadel*. (Boulder: Westview, 1990), 60.

viii Charles A. Moser, "The Achievement of Constance Garnett," *The American Scholar* 57 iss. 3 (1988), 431-438.